'I've been too much of a gentleman?

'Is that what you're trying to tell me?' Flynn asked.

Concealing her chagrin, Angie straightened and looked up at him with a serious expression. 'That's not what I meant at all. I've appreciated your behaviour. If you hadn't been a gentleman, I wouldn't have risked hiring you for tomorrow night's little scene.'

'I know.' He reached out to touch her cheek, his dark eyes unreadable in the shadows. 'If I hadn't been a gentleman for the past two days, you wouldn't have risked trusting me at all.

'But every gentleman has his limits,' Flynn went on softly.

STEPHANIE JAMES

is a pseudonym for bestselling, award-winning author **Jayne Ann Krentz**. Under various pseudonyms—including Jayne Castle and Amanda Quick—Ms. Krentz has over twenty-two million copies of her books in print. Her fans admire her versatility as she switches between historical, contemporary and futuristic romances. She attributes a 'lifelong addiction to romantic daydreaming' as the chief influence on her writing. With her husband, Frank, she currently resides in the Pacific Northwest.

Stephanie James

THE CHALLONER BRIDE

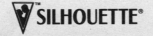
SILHOUETTE®

*Silhouette and Colophon are
registered trademarks of Harlequin Books S.A., used under licence.*

*First published in Great Britain 1987
Silhouette Books, Eton House, 18-24 Paradise Road,
Richmond, Surrey TW9 1SR*

© Jayne Ann Krentz 1987

ISBN 0 373 80690 6

104-9811

*Printed and bound in Spain
by Litografia Rosés S.A., Barcelona*

STEPHANIE JAMES COLLECTOR'S EDITION

Silhouette Books are delighted to have the opportunity
to present this selection of favourite titles from Stephanie
James, one of the world's most popular romance writers.
We hope that you will enjoy and treasure these attractive
Collector's Edition volumes and that they'll earn them-
selves a permanent place on your bookshelves.

TO TAME THE HUNTER
THE SILVER SNARE
THE CHALLONER BRIDE
THE DEVIL TO PAY
NIGHTWALKER
CAUTIOUS LOVER
SECOND WIFE
GREEN FIRE
NIGHT OF THE MAGICIAN
FABULOUS BEAST
GOLDEN GODDESS
WIZARD

One

There was undoubtedly an approved manner in which one went about hiring a professional soldier of fortune, but Angie Morgan didn't know what it was. The years she had put in after college doing personnel work hadn't provided any experience in that area. An engineer or a secretary or a new department head she could have managed with aplomb. This was a whole different matter.

At least she wasn't starting from scratch, she told herself as she watched Flynn Sangrey cross the floor of the open-air hotel lounge. She knew something about the man she was thinking of hiring. Enough, for example, to realize that she preferred the term "soldier of fortune" to the more realistic label of "mercenary."

Which was not to say that she knew him all that well. Two evenings spent sharing a couple of mar-

garitas while listening to a combo in a Mexican hotel nightclub hardly constituted an extensive relationship, let alone a job interview. On the other hand
how well did a woman really want to know a man
she was paying for protection? Surely it was better
to keep such acquaintances on a businesslike level.
When her business in Mexico was concluded, she
wasn't likely to see Sangrey again. From all indi-
cations he inhabited a much different world from her
own. Two ships passing in the night.

She wasn't absolutely positive that he made his
living as a mercenary. Her conclusion might simply
be the result of an overactive imagination. She had,
after all, very few hard facts. What convinced Angie
she wasn't far off base was the fact that Sangrey
had said nothing to counter her obvious assumptions, not even when she'd deliberately tried to give
him an opening to do so. Actually, he'd said almost
nothing concrete about himself, leaving her to draw
her own conclusions.

It wasn't easy to ask him personal questions; not
after knowing him for only two days. He had been
gravely polite since he'd introduced himself, but
somehow he'd made it clear he didn't invite detailed
probing. He was on vacation.

Sangrey threaded his way through the maze of
candlelit tables, moving with the kind of supple
masculine grace that spoke of coordination and
strength. It occurred to Angie that a mercenary's life
must be a hard one, hard enough to keep the body
of a man who was clearly on the far side of thirty-
five in shape.

He was dressed much as he had been for the past couple of days, in khaki shirt and dark twill slacks. The leather belt that circled his waist was utilitarian looking and rather worn. The leather moccasins he wore appeared to have been around awhile.

There was something in Sangrey's dark gaze that said he'd been around awhile, too. Angie had the impression that this man had seen some aspects of life that most people would prefer to ignore or forget. Only to be expected in his line of work, Angie told herself firmly. Julian would probably find him fascinating.

The rest of Sangrey went along with the image created by the tough, functional leather belt and the austere khaki shirt. He had probably never been very good looking, even before life had etched the hardness on his features. But tonight the flickering candlelight and the pale gleam of the stars overhead seemed to emphasize the fierce line of his nose and jaw. There was an aggressive, predatory element in Flynn Sangrey but Angie had the feeling it was well controlled. Everything about the man seemed controlled.

Maybe too controlled.

He hadn't even made a pass at her during the past two days.

Not that she wanted him to, Angie told herself instantly. After all, she was here in the Mexican Caribbean on business. She was definitely not interested in picking up a tall, dark stranger for the purpose of having a vacation fling. It was just vaguely disappointing that this particular tall, dark stranger hadn't seemed interested in picking her up, either. At least not for a quick, passionate fling. From the moment he had introduced himself two evenings ago, Angie had gained the distinct impression that Flynn Sangrey was only looking for a little casual companionship.

Perhaps he wouldn't be interested in a small job, either, she thought worriedly. The man was clearly treating himself to a vacation.

"Good evening."

Sangrey's voice was heavy, rather like the dark leather belt and the moccasins. Angie had grown to like it during the past couple of days. She smiled up at him as he took the chair beside her.

"How was the diving?" she asked, knowing that he had spent the afternoon in scuba gear.

"Unbelievable. The water around here is like crystal, and the fish swim along the reefs with you as if you're one of them. Another world." Flynn broke off to give his order to a passing waiter. Then he turned back to Angie, his dark gaze moving over her with polite, controlled interest. "How about you? Get that book finished?"

Angie shook her head, telling herself wistfully that his merely polite interest was probably generated by the fact that she wasn't Sangrey's fantasy of a vacation fling. Perhaps he had been hoping for something a little more exciting—maybe a flashy blonde who tended to spill out of her bikini.

Angie knew she was reasonably attractive, but she was definitely not flashy. Her dark brown hair was parted in the middle and coiled into a neat knot at the nape of her neck. It was a vaguely old-fashioned style that highlighted the odd blue-green color of her eyes.

Angie knew for a fact she was considered intelligent, hardworking and reliable. When she'd worked in personnel, she'd had access to all the evaluation forms, including her own. Since she'd gone to work for her uncle, nothing appeared to have changed. He seemed quite satisfied with her performance on the job. Angie wondered on a note of humor if the recommendation would impress Sangrey.

Her clothes were good but not trendy. She had a preference for a certain rakish look characterized by bold colors: black and white and red. Tonight she was wearing an off-the-shoulder, gauzy white cotton dress that was quite suitable for a trip to Mexico. The belt was the most striking feature of her attire. It was wide, neatly defining her small waist, and set with real garnets and gold filigree.

The belt was a clue, although the average person wasn't aware of it, to a deeply hidden streak of passion that ran through her nature like a fissure of gold through dark marble. On the surface, the overall image was cool and reserved, and Angie preferred to keep it that way. She didn't really trust that vein of temperamental gold she sensed within herself. It seemed a little alien to her, not fully understood or integrated into what she considered her real personality. A part of her didn't quite accept that hidden fissure; didn't know what to make of it. She sensed it could be dangerous, but by and large it didn't interfere with her daily life.

"I didn't get a chance to finish the book because I had a message from Alexander Cardinal," Angie announced as she picked up her drink.

Sangrey regarded her with polite interest. "The man you've been waiting to hear from? The one who lives on the island?"

"Uh-huh." Angie sipped the margarita, preparing to make her pitch. She had decided this afternoon to ask Sangrey if he would be interested in working for her. But she found herself somewhat nervous about actually broaching the question. "He sent word here to the hotel that he would see me tomorrow evening. He's invited me to dinner on the island. The message said he'd send a boat to pick me up."

Sangrey raised his eyebrows in mock admiration. "Classy. You move in the right circles, Angie."

"I explained yesterday that the circles aren't mine," she reminded him dryly. "My employer has set up this whole thing. Uncle Julian was supposed to make this trip himself. If he hadn't gotten sick at the last minute, I wouldn't even be here."

"Sounds to me like you've lucked out. A free trip to Mexico and dinner with a man who owns an island. Every woman's dream."

For the first time since she had met him, Angie found herself a little irritated with Flynn Sangrey. She didn't care for the faint derision in his tone. "Believe it or not, I have other things I'd rather be doing than sitting here in a hotel waiting on the convenience of a man who gives me very unpleasant chills down my spine!''

Sangrey lowered his lashes slightly, narrowing his dark gaze. ''What makes him so unpleasant? From what you've told me he's wealthy, a collector of art, and he commands a fair amount of respect from the locals. A guy who owns his own island can't be all bad.''

''I don't believe I told you exactly what it was he collected,'' Angie said grimly.

''I'm listening.''

''Weapons.''

Sangrey studied her for a few seconds. ''Weapons?''

Angie's mouth curved wryly. ''Not new ones, fortunately. At least not that I know of. He apparently has a thing for antique stuff. Old knives and pistols, that sort of thing. I'm hoping I won't find any M-16s hanging on the walls when I arrive for dinner.''

''You don't approve of Cardinal's collection?'' Flynn paid for his drink as it arrived, then leaned back in his chair to sip meditatively.

Angie flushed, wondering if she'd offended him in some oblique fashion. ''I realize that for a man in your, uh, profession, weapons collecting probably doesn't seem all that odd.''

He shrugged but said nothing.

''It's not just the fact that he collects things like that,'' Angie went on earnestly, ''it's the whole situation. Why would a man live in a fortress on an island that he owns if he hadn't made some unpleasant enemies in his life? Why retire down here in

Mexico? There's a lot of mystery about Alexander Cardinal's past and he makes me nervous. I'll bet he's a retired gangster or something. No wonder he likes old knives and things. He probably cut his teeth on a tommy gun.''

''Are you sure you're not letting your imagination run wild? What do you think he's going to do once he has you in his clutches? Assault you?''

''Of course not.'' Angie sighed, wondering how she was going to go about explaining her apprehension to a man who clearly didn't allow his imagination or anything else to get the best of him. ''I'm sure my uncle would never have sent me down here alone if he had any qualms about Mr. Cardinal. It's just that I feel, well, uncomfortable. Uneasy. Wary. I don't know. I don't like this job. I haven't liked it since Julian asked me to do it. Somehow I've lost my nerve.''

Flynn smiled fleetingly. ''Maybe you just need something to bolster your courage.''

Something in Angie responded to the brief dose of humor. ''Like another margarita?'' She stirred the one in front of her for a moment, thinking. ''You're right, of course. I am overreacting. Normally I'm quite efficient and businesslike about odd jobs such as this one. Heaven knows I get a lot of strange tasks from Uncle Julian. The variety is one of the reasons I've continued to work for him instead of going back into personnel. I don't know why this particular job is making me nervous.''

''Feminine intuition probably.''

"You don't sound as though you believe in intuition." She slanted Flynn an accusing glance.

"Oh, I believe in some forms of intuition," he retorted. "God knows I ought to, It's come in handy more than once in my life. But I've never been too certain about the feminine variety."

Angie's eyes lightened with humor. "That's because you're a man."

"I knew there had to be a simple explanation."

"Flynn?"

"Hmm?"

Angie cleared her throat softly, struggling to find the right words. "You said you were on vacation."

"Resting between engagements, I believe they say in the acting profession." He watched her over the rim of his glass.

"Yes, well, does that mean you have absolutely no interest in picking up a few quick bucks?" Angie questioned baldly.

There was a moment's silence from the other side of the table. When Flynn spoke his voice was so soft and dark Angie wasn't certain she'd heard him correctly.

"Is this a proposition?"

Aware of the sudden heat in her face, Angie shook her head angrily. "Don't be ridiculous. I'm offering you a temporary assignment. A job. Are you interested or not?"

"What, exactly, is the nature of the assignment?"

"Isn't it obvious?"

He made a small, dismissive gesture with his hand. "No."

"I would like an escort to Alexander Cardinal's island tomorrow evening. There, is that clear enough? You'll be well paid. My uncle never questions my expense accounts." How could he? She prepared and paid all of her own expense accounts. Then she handed them over to Julian's accountant. Julian didn't want to be bothered with petty details.

"Then this offer is in the nature of a proposition?" There was a hard edge underlying Flynn's words.

"This offer," Angie said feelingly, "is a request for your services as a bodyguard!"

He blinked, the slow, speculative blink of a large night animal. "You really are nervous, aren't you?"

"Yes." She waited, an element of challenge in her eyes.

Sangrey considered the matter for a long moment. "Will Cardinal allow you to bring a guest along tomorrow evening?"

"I don't see why not. There was nothing said about having to go alone. I'm sure if I just show up with you in tow and act as though I had understood the invitation to include my *friend,* he'll be polite about the whole thing. I've heard he prides himself on his good manners. Julian assured me Cardinal appears to be a gentleman. He's been corresponding with him for some time."

"Yet you're scared of the man?"

Angie smiled ruefully. "I know it doesn't sound rational."

"Feminine intuition?"

"I'm afraid so. Or maybe just plain old nerves." She waited a few seconds. "Are you interested?"

Flynn lifted one shoulder in casual acceptance. "Why not? It sounds like it could be an interesting evening."

Angie drew in a slow breath as something occurred to her. "I hope you and Mr. Cardinal won't have too much in common."

"Not likely. I don't have his kind of money. Or an island."

The sarcasm annoyed Angie. "I was referring to a mutual interest in weapons and related activities," she said caustically.

"If you didn't believe I had an interest in that sort of thing you wouldn't be wanting to hire me as an escort, would you?" Flynn countered with unassailable logic.

Angie winced and chose to alter the direction of the conversation. "How much?"

He looked blank. "How much what?"

"How much do you charge? Is there an hourly or daily rate? I've never hired someone like you before. I don't really know how to handle the business side of things."

"Someone like me," he repeated slowly. "How much do you know about people like me, Angie?"

"Very little," she admitted.

"Remember that."

"Look, if you're going to go all cryptic and enigmatic on me, let's just forget the whole thing. With Alexander Cardinal hovering in the background, the last thing I need is another man around who makes me nervous!''

Unexpectedly Flynn chuckled. ''I'll try to avoid that.''

''Then it's settled?''

''It's settled. You look very relieved.''

''I am,'' she confirmed. ''But you haven't told me how much you, er, charge yet.''

''I'll have to think about it.''

The practical side of Angie's nature intruded. ''Don't think too hard about it. I'm planning to list your services under 'miscellaneous expenses' when it comes time to itemize the costs of this trip, so I hope you'll keep your charges reasonable.''

''Miscellaneous expenses.'' He played with the word as he said it, his gaze full of sardonic humor. ''Somehow that sounds so unimportant. So vague. Kind of uninteresting. Do you find me uninteresting and vague, Angie?''

She wasn't quite sure how to take his teasing. ''Not any more uninteresting and vague than you probably find me,'' she assured him cheerfully.

Flynn set his glass down and leaned forward to bracket the drink with his elbows. His hands splayed wide on the polished black surface of the cocktail table. At the tips of his fingers the candle burned in its amber dish. He smiled.

''I find you fascinating, Angie. I'm looking forward to working for you and with you tomorrow night.''

''You are?'' Her skepticism probably showed. But she couldn't deny that his words created a pleasurable stir of excitement deep within her. Her eyes went to his hands. They were large hands with strong wrists and blunt fingers. A tiny shiver went through her as, involuntarily, she wondered what those hands would feel like on her body.

"Will you dance with me, Angie?"

She started a little, wondering if he'd just read her mind. It was the first time he'd asked her to dance. Without a word she inclined her head in aloof agreement. Flynn led her out onto the floor and took her into his arms. His big, powerful hands closed around her and Angie had the answer to her question. His hands felt good. Strong and warm and good. They felt right.

She was aware of the strength in his grasp, but she also sensed the control behind that strength. Angie relaxed into the rhythm of the dance, allowing herself to follow Flynn's smooth, controlled lead. Overhead the stars gleamed in the black velvet night, and the balmy air was scented with the sea. Around Angie the other dancers seemed totally absorbed in themselves. She felt alone with the man who held her. It gave her the courage to risk a personal question.

"Flynn?"

"Hmm?" His voice came from the region of her right ear. His mouth almost touched her hair.

"How long will you be staying here?"

"In Mexico? A few days. It depends."

Angie wondered what it depended on and didn't know how to ask. Part of her reticence was created by the fact that she didn't really want to know for certain how he made his living. She shied away from hearing the truth stated openly. It was unpleasant enough to assume that he was a mercenary; knowing for certain would be painful. Men who worked at the business of fighting other people's wars had an ancient and established calling. It was not, however, a particularly pleasant or respected calling. And it was definitely not a profession that encouraged long-range personal planning.

"I just wondered," she whispered. The scent of him was curiously intriguing, unlike anything Angie had ever experienced. She turned her nose unobtrusively into his shoulder and teased herself with the aroma of hotel soap and honest male sweat.

"Will you be leaving after you've made your deal with Cardinal?" Flynn asked into her hair.

"Yes. Unlike you, I'm not really on vacation. Besides, I don't want to be responsible for that damn dagger for too long."

"Dagger?" One large palm flexed at the base of Angie's spine. Flynn's strong fingers sank briefly into her skin and then relaxed. "That's what you're going to get from Cardinal?"

"I told you he collected weapons." Angie wondered if the movement of his hand on her back had been deliberate or only a reflexive motion. In either event it had elicited a small tremor of excitement and she half hoped he would do it again.

"Your employer collects weapons, too? Is that why you're down here negotiating for a dagger?"

She didn't really want to talk about the deal, but now that she'd involved him it seemed only fair to give Flynn some of the facts. With a small, stifled sigh of regret Angie lifted her head to meet his gaze. He was watching her intently.

"Julian doesn't collect weapons," she assured him. "Just this one particular dagger. It's very old, apparently. Dates back to the late seventeen hundreds. It once belonged to Julian's family, you see. The Torres family."

Sangrey's fingers moved again in that flexing motion at the base of her spine. "You said Julian is your uncle. That means the dagger was once in *your* family."

"Well, I suppose so if you want to get technical. Frankly, I've never paid too much attention to the past. I've never had an interest in genealogy or family traditions. Life is for living in the present and the future." She smiled gently. "I imagine a man in your line of work understands that."

He looked down at her as though he were about to say something and then he changed his mind. "Tell me more about the dagger."

"There's not much to tell. It disappeared a long time ago. Over the years it went through a variety of hands, but several months ago Julian had it traced to the Cardinal collection. He opened negotiations with Alexander Cardinal, who, surprisingly, agreed to sell. I guess Uncle Julian appealed to him on the grounds of family tradition, and Cardinal seemed to understand my uncle's desire to have the dagger back in the family."

Again Flynn's hand moved on her back and again

Angie couldn't tell if the touch was deliberate or casual.

"And now you've come to collect the dagger and take it back to your uncle," Flynn observed. "It must be valuable."

Angie considered that. "I suppose it is, but not extravagantly so. It's no dollar-ninety-eight pocketknife, but it's not exactly Excalibur, either. Julian tells me the blade is of Damascus steel and there is an intricately worked handle. I think the pommel is set with some semiprecious stones." She laughed lightly. "The thing's not made of diamonds and gold. The real value of the dagger to Julian is sentimental."

"You don't sound as if you approve of that sort of sentiment."

"Oh, I'm not hardhearted about it. I'm glad my uncle is finally getting his hands on the dagger. It's something he's been working on for a long time."

"When did Julian lose the thing?" Flynn sounded vaguely irritated.

"He didn't lose it. It was lost years ago by the family that was responsible for keeping track of it." Angie felt a flash of irritation, too, as she jumped to her uncle's defense. She frowned. "I've told you Julian's last name is Torres. He's the last male descendant of an old Spanish family that once held a lot of land in California. The dagger is called the Torres Dagger. It's a long story."

"I'm listening."

Angie tilted her head to one side. "You really want to hear the tale of the dagger?"

"I can't think of anything else I'd rather do than listen to it."

Thanks a lot, Angie thought grimly. She could think of several other things she'd rather be doing at the moment. A walk in the hotel gardens, a long, intimate discussion of the future, a soft kiss down on the beach. Hundreds of other things. But apparently Flynn didn't feel the same way. Firmly Angie reminded herself once again that it made more sense to keep her relationship with Flynn Sangrey on a polite, platonic level.

"Well, according to Julian the dagger originally belonged to a distant ancestress of ours, a beautiful Spanish woman named Maria Isabel. It seems that there was a feud going on between the Torres family and the Challoners, the family that owned the ranch that bordered Torres land in California. A dispute over a large chunk of property. Nothing gets landholding people more upset than an argument over who owns what, I guess. At any rate, according to the story the altercation was settled in the time-honored way."

"All-out war?"

Angie shook her head, smiling. "Only for a while. Then the Challoners presented an alternative solution: a marriage alliance. The head of the Challoner clan offered to marry the eldest Torres daughter, poor Maria Isabel. The disputed hunk of ground would be her dowry and would descend through her to her children. Both families would be linked to the land they coveted."

"Why do you call Maria Isabel poor? It sounds like a reasonable solution to me."

"Typical male approach to the problem." Angie shot Flynn a disgusted glance. "Just use a convenient daughter to seal the bargain and settle the matter of land title. Never mind what the poor daughter happens to think about the situation."

"I take it Maria Isabel objected to the solution?" Flynn asked dryly.

"Most vehemently, according to the legend. She stormed and argued for days, but her father was one of those old-style domineering patriarchs. He'd accepted the offer of marriage from his neighbor and his daughter was going to go through with the deal come hell or high water." Angie shuddered.

"I wouldn't waste too much time empathizing with Maria Isabel if I were you. She was a woman of her time, and that was the way things were done back then."

"With that attitude I think you would have done very well yourself in those days," Angie muttered. "I can't imagine putting a woman through such anguish for the sake of settling a land dispute!"

"It seems perfectly reasonable to me. In those days the power of a family was directly proportional to the land it held. It was crucial to maintain control over as much territory as possible. What did the tantrums of a sulking daughter matter compared to forming an important alliance?"

Angie glowered up at him. "If you want to hear the rest of the story, you'd better cease and desist offering opinions on the rights and wrongs of the situation!''

Flynn's fingers moved once more just above the curve of her hips and he smiled wryly. ''I get the message. Finish the story.''

''Well, according to Julian, who had the tale from his father, who got it handed down from his father, et cetera, et cetera, Maria Isabel finally told her parents she would surrender to the inevitable.''

''Smart woman.''

Angie ignored that. ''But she had plans of her own. On her wedding night she concealed the Torres Dagger in her gown.''

''I take it back. Not such a smart woman after all.''

Angie sighed. ''Actually, it sounds like a logical thing to do under the circumstances.''

''Bring a dagger to your wedding bed?'' Something feral gleamed for a moment in Flynn's eyes.

''It's obvious you're never going to understand the woman's side of the tale.''

''Finish it,'' Flynn instructed.

''There's not much more to tell,'' Angie admitted. ''No one really knows what happened on the wedding night.''

''Maria Isabel's new husband didn't wake up dead, did he?''

''Well, no.''

''And Maria Isabel survived, too?''

Angie nodded. ''According to the story they were both very much alive the next morning. Maria Isabel and her husband had seven children during the years that followed.''

"Then I think it's safe to assume Maria Isabel had her mind changed for her on her wedding night.'' Flynn's mouth curved laconically. "You want me to guess what happened?''

Angie laughed in spite of herself. "I can imagine what a man would assume happened that night. Your guess is that Maria Isabel's new husband disarmed her with mad, passionate love, right?''

"No, I have a hunch the mad, passionate love came later. My guess is he disarmed her very forcefully, without any love at all. He was probably madder than hell.''

Angie's amusement faded. "It doesn't sound like an auspicious beginning for a marriage.''

"Oh, I don't know.'' Flynn sounded suddenly philosophical. "It undoubtedly served to lay out the ground rules in no uncertain terms. Since no-fault divorce laws didn't exist back then, it was probably important to settle the critical issues early on in a marriage. And any bride who shows up on her wedding night with a dagger in her nightgown needs a firm hand right from the start.''

Angie's eyes narrowed. Then she reminded herself that it was merely a legend about a very distant relation and didn't affect the present at all. There was absolutely no reason why she should feel obliged to defend Maria Isabel at this late date. "Well, whatever the real story is of what happened that night, the rest of the dagger's tale is known. Julian says that the morning after the wedding the

Torres Dagger was hung in state over the fireplace in the master bedroom of Maria Isabel's new home. It remained there for several generations, during which time both families prospered. Apparently the Torreses and the Challoners began to see the dagger as a symbol of good luck for both families. But sometime in the early 1900s the dagger disappeared. And with it, apparently, the good luck of both families."

"What happened?"

Angie shrugged. "Julian says that after the dagger disappeared, the families began to dwindle and die out. The power and money faded. The land itself was lost during the 1920s. It's been divided up among a lot of different owners. Some of it's farmland and some of it's subdivisions now. Julian managed to buy back the site of the old Torres hacienda, though. He's had a new house built in the Spanish colonial style. And there's a charming little guest cottage, too. That's where I live. I got to move in a few weeks ago, but Julian isn't scheduled to move into the hacienda itself until next month."

"Are you and Julian about the last of the Torres line?" Flynn asked carefully.

"Well, there's my mother, Julian's sister, but I was her only child. She and my father divorced several years ago and she moved east. My uncle has never married. He's in his sixties now. He asked me to become his research assistant a couple of years ago. From what we can tell with genealogical research, there aren't any other Torres relations around. He and I and my mother are all that's left."

"What about the other family? The one Maria Isabel married into."

"Julian thinks there's a possibility that somewhere a descendant of the Challoners is still alive, but he has no way of knowing for certain. He's made a few attempts to trace the family, and the most he can determine is that there were two Challoner brothers in service in World War II. One didn't survive. The other returned and married and there may have been children. Julian wasn't able to trace the family any further. After all these years it doesn't much matter."

"It sounds to me like it matters a whole lot," Flynn growled. "If one of Maria Isabel's descendants is alive, the dagger belongs to him."

Angie's brows came together in a fierce line above her nose. "You're beginning to sound as bad as Julian! For heaven's sake, we all live in the present, not the past. That dagger belongs only to whoever happens to purchase it next. In this case, that purchaser is Julian Torres."

"The dagger symbolizes something important, Angie. You told me yourself, it brought luck to two families for several generations. It represented the land and the power of those two families."

"Good grief! That's just a legend. Everyone is responsible for making his or her own luck in this world. I should think you, of all people, would understand that. You look as if you've been making your own way for some time."

"That doesn't mean I don't understand the value of traditions and legends," Flynn countered softly.

"Doesn't the tale of that dagger mean anything to you?"

"Not particularly. It's an interesting story but that's all it is to me: a story."

He looked down at her searchingly. "You're connected to that dagger and its history. Don't you have any feeling for your past?"

She laughed up at him, amused by his unexpectedly serious attitude toward the subject. "Flynn, you are looking at a thoroughly modern Californian. A child of the present. Before I went to work for Uncle Julian, I couldn't name anyone farther back on my family tree than my grandparents! And the only reason I can do a little better now is because Uncle Julian has made me help him out on some of his genealogical research."

"But that research is just a job to you, isn't it?"

"You've got it. I much prefer the here and now. What good does it do to dwell on the distant past? There's nothing to be gained or changed. Tracking down family legends makes an interesting hobby for someone like my uncle, I suppose, but that's about it."

"But in this case the family legend represents a lot more than just an amusing tale. From what you've said, the dagger was a link between two families and the land that gave them their power. Something important was lost when that dagger disappeared. If you'd spent as much time living in strange places as I have, you might have more appreciation for the importance of families and their legends. There are places in this world where the family tie

is the most crucial tie there is. Families are how
people become immortal, Angie.''

"I'm really not interested in building family dy-
nasties,'' she temporized dryly. ''It's probably more
of a male fantasy, anyway, since lines of descent are
usually through the male surname. Men sometimes
have this thing about achieving immortality through
their descendants.''

"I wouldn't call a man's desire to establish a
strong, lasting family a fantasy!''

"I would. It was undoubtedly the old-fashioned
equivalent of heading up a corporation. A form of
power.''

"There's nothing wrong in a man's search for
power and strength and nothing wrong in his wish
to hand that power and strength down to the next
generation. It's a survival instinct.

Angie smiled very brightly. ''Well, I certainly
don't share that instinct. As a woman, I would resent
being used to cement a dynasty. I can understand
exactly how Maria Isabel must have felt. But I can't
quite figure out why we're arguing about the matter.
You don't seem to subscribe to that sort of male
fantasy. If you did you would be back in the States
working day and night to build a ranch or a corporation or something. You'd be worrying about marrying a woman who could bring you a dowry and
give you lots of sons, not vacationing alone in Mexico.''

Flynn's mouth curved abruptly and his gaze
warmed. ''I'm not vacationing alone. I'm with
you.''

Angie's breath caught for a split second. "Yes," she whispered. "Yes, you are."

Flynn stopped, his hand sliding more aggressively around her waist. "Let's go outside for a few minutes."

"Why?" Angie felt a tremor of excitement rush through her. It was followed almost instantly by a shiver of sensual alarm when Flynn didn't answer. The two conflicting sensations confused her for a moment, and by the time she recovered she found herself out in the gardens that fronted the night-darkened sea.

They walked in silence for several minutes. The scent of the ocean air mingled with the aromas of the exotic tropical garden, creating an impression of timeless fantasy. Angie was vividly aware of the man beside her. It occurred to her that part of her had been aware of him on this sensual level since the first moment they'd met.

"Will you be going back to the States the day after tomorrow?" Flynn came to a halt beside a stone wall that had been built to separate the hotel gardens from the beach.

"I should leave as soon as possible. I told you, for me this isn't really supposed to be a vacation." Angie put her hand on the waist-high wall. The stones were still warm from the sun. "What about you? How long will you be 'resting between engagements'?"

His shoulders moved in the darkness, a casual shrug that told her nothing. "I haven't decided."

There was silence between them again. There had

often been silences during the past couple of days. At times Flynn was very difficult to communicate with, Angie reflected. At other times, and they were the majority, the conversation flowed between them as naturally as the tides. She leaned forward, resting her arms on the stone wall, and gazed out toward the sea. "You know, somehow you're not quite what I would have expected."

"What would you expect?" There was a thread of amusement in the words.

"I don't know. I've never met a man who made his living the way I think you make yours." The impulse toward honesty surprised her. For two days she had deliberately not pushed too hard to answers. She realized now that she'd been half afraid of the ones she might get. "But if I'd thought about it, I'd have guessed that a man in your situation might be far more, uh, aggressive with a woman than you've been. Especially when he was on vacation. A sort of live-for-the-moment syndrome. Eat, drink and be merry. Wine, women and song."

"Are you by any chance trying to tell me in a very delicate way that I've been too much of a gentleman?" Flynn sounded more amused than ever.

Concealing her chagrin, Angie straightened away from the wall and looked up at him with a serious expression. "That's not what I meant at all. I've appreciated your behavior. If you hadn't been a gentleman, I wouldn't have risked hiring you for tomorrow night's little scene."

"I know." He reached out to touch the side of her cheek, his dark eyes unreadable in the shadows.

''If I hadn't been a gentleman for the past two days, you wouldn't have risked trusting me at all. And it was very important that you trust me.''

''Flynn?''

''But every gentleman has his limits,'' Flynn went on softly. He slid his large hand behind her head and tilted her face up so that starlight illuminated the questions in her eyes. ''And I think I'm reaching mine.''

He brought his mouth down to hers before Angie could find the words to stop him.

Two

He'd seen the sensual awareness in her eyes the moment he'd introduced himself. It had pleased him. More than that, it had filled him with a curious sense of anticipation. He could and would use that awareness, Flynn had told himself. He would use whatever worked. He was too close now to let anything stand in his way.

Flynn felt Angie shiver delicately beneath his hand as his mouth found hers. The sensation sent a ripple of raw excitement through him. It had been clear for the past two days that the awareness in Angie was controlled with an ample amount of feminine caution and common sense. But he sensed that there was a well of passion to be tapped if the right man took his time and planned carefully. It was very satisfying to lure her over those high, self-imposed barriers and into the lush green fields of temptation.

Flynn realized he had been waiting for this moment for the past forty-eight hours.

It had been difficult playing the casual, scrupulously polite gentleman for two days, especially here, where they were enveloped in the exotic, carefree atmosphere of the luxurious tropical resort. If he hadn't had more important goals on his mind, Flynn knew he would have made the pass Angie had expected the first night. He had found himself wanting to spend every waking moment with her, trying to impress himself on her consciousness.

But Flynn had hunted long enough to know that the cautious, careful quarry was most efficiently trapped through its own natural curiosity. Keeping his distance had netted him much faster and more useful results than he would have obtained through the direct approach. Angie's offer of a job tonight had told him that much.

It was all enough to make a man believe in fate, Flynn decided triumphantly as he ran the tip of his tongue along Angie's lower lip. Her mouth quivered and opened beneath the tantalizing caress. With a groan of mounting desire Flynn accepted the soft invitation.

He explored the warm, intimate darkness behind her lips, and his body began demanding the completion of the ancient formula. He hadn't planned on more than a kiss this evening. It was crucial not to alarm Angie at this stage. Flynn reminded himself that his ultimate goal was far more important than a night in bed with a woman. He knew his self-control was formidable, and he had great confidence in it.

But he couldn't stop himself from teasing the sensitive nape of Angie's neck, and when she sighed softly in response he found himself touching her just above the low neckline of her dress. She wasn't wearing a bra. Flynn urged her closer so that he could feel the gentle thrust of her breasts against his chest.

It was delicious. She made a tiny sound at the back of her throat and her fingertips closed over his shoulders. He was vividly aware of the firm peaks of her nipples and knew a sudden, fierce desire to test them with his palm.

She was so sweetly responsive, he thought. And he felt dazed by the elemental sense of power that was surging through him now. She was twenty-eight, and God knew he was getting perilously close to forty. At this stage both of them should be capable of choreographing their responses with far more finesse. It was unexpected and unsettling to find his sense of control threatened already.

Flynn knew matters were getting dangerous when he found himself sliding a probing finger inside the elasticized neckline of Angie's white dress. She stilled for a moment in his arms, and he told himself he'd better stop. It had gone far enough. The last thing he wanted to do tonight was push too fast or too hard. It would be far more effective to arouse her gently and leave her wanting him.

Easy does it, he told himself determinedly. *This is where it stops. Any further and you start risking her trust. There's too much of a chance she'll pull back and become cautious again.* And there was too much at stake to lose the advantage he had gained during the past two days.

But his hand seemed to move of its own volition and the gauzy white dress slipped downward.

"Flynn..." Angie's eyes were closed. Her nails bit into the fabric of the khaki shirt. "I don't think we should let this go any further...."

"I know. Believe me, honey, I know." But now that he was so close to touching the hardened tips of her breasts, he didn't want to stop. "Just let me see you for a moment. I want to know what the moonlight looks like on your skin." He took a breath and with both hands pushed the elasticized material down to her waist.

For an instant she stood trapped before him, her wrists caught and tangled in the sleeves of the dress. Her lashes lifted and she met his eyes. Flynn found himself staring.

"Angie," he grated. His hands lifted to cup the small, rounded fullness of her breasts. She was delicately constructed, her body slender but softened with curves at breast and thigh. "Angie, you're lovely."

"So are you." She freed her hands and wrapped her arms around his neck. Then she put her lips to the tanned skin of his throat and pressed gently against him. "Oh, Flynn. So are you."

It was okay, Flynn heard a hammering voice in his veins say. It was all right. He wouldn't endanger his ultimate goal by making love to Angie tonight.

No problem. She wanted him. She would come to him as easily as a bird to its nest. All he had to do was lead her back to his room, lock the door and lay her down on his bed. In his head he could see her there already.

The heat in his body seemed to be leaping out of control. Flynn grazed the tips of Angie's breasts with his palms and then slipped his hands around her to find the line of her spine.

Below on the beach the waves lapped at the sand in a primitive rhythm that echoed the heavy beat of his blood. Everything in his mind that was not directly connected with Angie began to recede into the distance. In a vague way he tried to remind himself of his purpose in being here, but he was already deciding it could wait until morning.

Everything except Angie could wait until morning.

"Come with me." His voice sounded rough to his own ears. He wished he could make it smooth and liquid. "Come with me, Angie. I want you tonight. I'll make it good for you. I swear it. I'll do whatever it takes to make it perfect. Angie, let's go back. Come with me, honey...."

He felt her shudder against him, and then she was pulling free. Her reluctance was obvious, but so was the somewhat dazed determination in her face. She looked up at him as her hands slid down his chest and slowly she shook her head.

"I'm sorry, Flynn. It's too soon. I should never have let things go this far. Please forgive me for leading you on." Her smile was tremulous, her eyes wide and pleading. "I'm supposed to be here on business, not for a romantic fling. I got a little carried away, I guess." Hastily she adjusted her dress, turning toward the sea as she pulled the material back up over her shoulders.

Behind her Flynn took a couple of slow breaths, aware that his hands were in fists at his sides. His whole body felt coiled and tense. She couldn't just call a halt like this. Could she? He'd felt her response; knew she wanted him. Damn it, he was the one who was supposed to be directing this scene.

"Relax, Angie. It's all right. You don't have to be afraid of me." It was a struggle to find the words. He wanted to pick her up and carry her back to his room and forget words altogether.

She glanced back at him over her shoulder. The moonlight illuminated her profile. Her eyes seemed very large and strangely colorless in the night light. "I'm not afraid of you, Flynn. I haven't been afraid of you since the moment we met."

"Angie, please. I want you to trust me."

"I do trust you." She smiled again and put out a hand to touch his sleeve. "It's myself and the situation I don't trust. This can't go anywhere, can it, Flynn? I'll be on my way home the day after tomorrow. And you...you'll be on your way back to wherever men in your profession are finding work these days. That probably takes in a good portion of the globe, doesn't it?"

"Is it what I do for a living that bothers you?" he asked starkly, knowing she had skirted the issue more than once during the past couple of days.

"It's not any of my business." Her hand fell away from his arm. "But I'm not a good candidate for a one-night stand, Flynn." Her mouth curved in wry humor. "I'd probably whine a lot the next morning. You know, throw a tantrum and hurl recriminations. That sort of thing. The last thing you need while you're on vacation is a woman who stages a major scene at the airport when you're trying to say goodbye. It would be better for both of us if we kept this relationship businesslike."

The sleek edge of anger knifed through him unexpectedly. That was supposed to be his line, Flynn thought savagely. He was the one who had been keeping things carefully poised on the brink between business and pleasure. He'd been doing it deliberately, using the resulting tension to attract his quarry. And now the quarry was using it against him. Hurriedly he sought for a way to recover his strategic position.

"Don't worry, Angie. The last thing I want to do is push you into something you don't want."

"It's not that I don't want—" she began urgently.

"I understand." He smiled as he cut off her small attempt to explain. "No problem." Then he stepped forward and took her arm to guide her back through the moonlit gardens. He was okay now. Back under control. "A kiss overlooking the beach is the perfect finishing touch to the evening, don't you think? What time are you going to breakfast in the morning?"

She looked as if she wanted to say something else but couldn't think of any way to get the conversation back on its original track. "About seven. Same time as this morning."

"Sounds good. I'll see you then."

"You're still interested in coming with me to-morrow evening?" she asked tentatively.

"How can I turn down such an easy assign-ment?" He grinned as they walked back into the main lobby of the hotel. "A free meal and a cruise on the bay. Sounds great."

"I really do appreciate it, Flynn. I know there's no logical reason to be nervous."

"But you are. Don't apologize. There's no need." He walked her into the elevator and down the hall to her second-floor room.

When he halted in front of her door, Angie turned to look up at him with a questioning expression. "Good night, Flynn. And thank you. For every-thing."

He bent his head and brushed his mouth against her lips. "My pleasure. See you in the morning."

He forced himself not to linger over the kiss. An-gie hesitated as if trying to decide what to do next, but as he just stood politely, waiting, she quickly turned the key in the lock and stepped inside the room.

As soon as the door closed in his face, the politely reassuring smile Flynn had been wearing vanished. He swung around, then stalked down the hall to the elevator and punched the button.

"Stupid, stupid, stupid." Leaning against the wall, arms folded, he muttered the words in a soft, disgusted litany. He'd been on the verge of risking everything for the sake of a night in bed with Angie Morgan. It made no sense. His entire goal hinged on keeping her trust and friendship. A little sexual attraction was a bonus to be used wisely. He'd almost thrown away the trust and friendship by trying to sweep her into bed.

There was no doubt he would have taken a lot of satisfaction in making love to her, and Flynn was almost certain he could have made her enjoy the experience, too. But there was too much risk involved. Angie was right, she wasn't a good candidate for a one-night stand. He might have been able to coax her into bed this evening, but he couldn't know what her reaction would be in the morning. She might, indeed, wake up full of recriminations, just as she had suggested.

Worse yet, she might have been so nervous around him that she would have retracted her job offer. Since he'd spent the past two days feeding her the notion that she would feel more comfortable with him along tomorrow evening, it would be a pity to scare her off now.

"Sangrey, you're a damn fool." The elevator doors slid open and Flynn stepped inside. The car was empty and he rode it up to the next floor thinking of Angie's eyes. He'd been half-consciously trying to figure out what color they were and tonight it came to him. She had eyes the color of a peacock's feathers.

Dusk shrouded the bay the next evening as the launch cut through the water with a subdued roar.

Angie sat in the back, her hair shielded from the breeze by a silk scarf. At the helm a taciturn man dressed in white trousers and a white, military-style shirt guided the boat toward Cardinal's private island.

Behind her the lights of the beachfront hotel began to wink into existence. A tiny village that skirted the hotel dotted the beach with a few more lights, but there was little else to relieve the darkness. This portion of the Mexican coastline was uninhabited for long stretches. It was an area the government was just beginning to develop for tourists, and as yet there were few signs of civilization near the resort.

Angie had decided to wear a yellow-and-turquoise silk chemise tonight. When she saw the crisply attired launch pilot, she was glad she had. Alexander Cardinal was clearly a man who valued a certain degree of formality. Beside her, Flynn was dressed in his usual fashion: an open-throated shirt and close-fitting pants. The shirt was black tonight and the pants were charcoal gray. He had on the familiar worn leather belt and moccasins. The only concession to formality was the light-colored sports jacket that lay flung over the seat in front of him. Perhaps moccasins and a sports jacket were de rigueur in the various places around the world where he went to make his living.

In that moment Angie didn't care what he wore. She was just glad he was along for the ride. None of her uneasiness was diminishing as the launch approached Cardinal's island. When she felt Flynn's hand close lightly over her fingers, she realized he was aware of her wariness. She turned her head to smile at him.

He smiled back, but didn't try to shout above the roar of the launch's motor. The balmy breeze rippled the black pelt of his hair. Angie reflected briefly that with his dark hair and eyes he might have had a Spanish ancestor somewhere on the family tree.

She felt the impact of the dark gaze as he watched her and found herself flushing a bit. Firmly she focused her attention on the small island they were approaching. Matters had been friendly, polite and casual between herself and Flynn all day today. She knew it was best to keep them that way.

But knowing that that was the wisest course had not deterred her from thinking about him for a long time before she went to sleep the night before. The memory of his large, strong hands on her body had ignited a sensual warmth in her that had taken a long time to fade. Her curiosity about what it would feel like to have him touch her had been partially satisfied, but the answers had only created more wonder and more curiosity.

She was relieved that he had been so willing to allow her to call a halt in the garden. A part of her had been uncertain of just how cooperative he would be in a situation such as that. After all, a man in his line of work undoubtedly had to take his pleasures where he could or risk losing them.

His line of work. The words echoed again in her mind as the launch pilot guided the boat into small, shallow bay on Cardinal's island. It was strange how neither Flynn nor herself ever mentioned his work directly in their conversations. He had told her about his visits to some strange, troubled places, but he hadn't actually mentioned what he did while he was there.

Angie hadn't asked. She had guessed his profession soon after meeting him. There was a toughness in him that she knew intuitively went to the bone. The sometimes cynical, often laconic, fundamentally unyielding expression in his dark eyes was not the look of a stockbroker or interior designer on vacation. Everything about Flynn Sangrey warned that he knew too much about the violent side of life.

And since Angie didn't want to think about how completely separate his world was from her own, she didn't ask him directly about his profession.

She wondered if it was hypocritical of her to have asked Flynn for his services this evening.

Before she could struggle with the ethics of the situation, the pilot had the launch tied up at the dock. Nearby rocked a gleaming white yacht that must have been in the neighborhood of fifty to sixty feet. On the hull, black letters spelled out the name: *Cardinal Rule.*

"At least the guy seems to have a sense of humor," Flynn observed as he handed Angie up out of the launch.

"Either that or an ego problem." Angie removed her scarf and turned to smile blandly at the silent launch pilot. "Thank you," she murmured as he politely indicated the steps leading up to a formal garden. He didn't return her smile.

She stood for a moment looking at the villa that

dominated the extensive gardens. A rich man's retreat in paradise, she thought, surveying the cool fountains, wide terraces and pristine white walls. Beyond the gardens palm trees swayed in the evening breeze.

"Julian's going to be sorry he missed this," Angie whispered to Flynn. "It would have been a perfect setting for a book."

"Julian writes?"

"Umm. But not under his own name. He uses the pen name Julian Taylor."

Beside her, Flynn cocked one black brow. "That sounds vaguely familiar."

Angie hid a smile. "He's the author of a series of very popular men's adventure novels featuring a character named Jake Savage. There's one out every six months or so. Translated into eight languages. I don't imagine you read that sort of thing."

Flynn frowned briefly as he walked beside her up the stone path that wound through the garden. The launch pilot was silently leading the way toward the front doors of the villa. "Some series about a guy who free-lances?"

"Free-lances?" Angie repeated.

Flynn made a cutting movement with his hand. "You know, hires himself out to people who are willing to pay for services rendered." The dark eyes flickered. "Like I'm doing tonight."

Angie took a deep breath, never having thought of Jake Savage as a mercenary. But of course that was what he was.

"I suppose you could say that. How many books have you read in the Savage series?"

Flynn shrugged. "Only one. It wasn't bad technically."

"I beg your pardon?"

"Technically. It was okay technically." He gave her an impatient glance.

"You mean grammatically and structurally it was good?" She was rather surprised that he had bothered to dissect it in those terms. Most people who read the Savage series were looking for action and adventure, not writing expertise.

"I mean," Flynn explained as if she weren't very bright, "that the technical details were good. The descriptions of the weapons and how they handled were fairly accurate."

"Oh." Yes, of course. *Technically.* The word obviously had different meanings to different people.

Before Angie could think of anything else to say, the doors of the villa swung open. Standing on the threshold was a short, powerfully built man who reminded Angie of a gorilla in evening clothes. She nearly missed her footing on the first step. Instantly Flynn's hand was under her arm, steadying her. He appeared completely unconcerned by the sight of the big man in the doorway.

"Miss Morgan and her friend," the launch pilot announced briskly. Then he turned and headed back down toward the docks.

The man in the doorway nodded formally. "Mr. Cardinal is expecting you," he said gravely to Angie. Then he looked speculatively at Flynn. "We didn't realize you were bringing a friend."

"Flynn Sangrey." Flynn announced himself easily and waited, not volunteering further explanation.

"This way, please." The gorilla stepped aside and beckoned them into the white tiled hall. "Mr. Cardinal is on the west terrace."

Angie found herself keeping close to Flynn as they followed the man ahead of them. She swept the elegantly cool interior of the villa with a fascinated gaze. Julian had a more accurate eye for such details, but she was willing to bet that the abstract art on the walls was original. The tile beneath her feet probably came from Italy, and the Oriental rugs were definitely not reproductions. More than ever she wondered what sort of business Alexander Cardinal was in. Or had once been in. The gorilla came to a halt at a point where French doors stood open onto a terrace.

"Miss Morgan and her *friend,* Mr. Sangrey."

"Thank you, Haslett." Alexander Cardinal rose from the white wicker chair in which he had been sitting and came forward.

He was rather as Angie had expected. He looked perfectly at home in the tropical fantasy surrounding him. Tall, athletically lean, Cardinal was a man in his late sixties. His features were aristocratic; the eyes piercingly blue. His hair was blazingly white, and he still had most of it. The white linen tropical suit he wore had obviously been tailor-made. Everything about him was elegantly refined and infinitely charming. Angie found herself mentally casting him in a film about a wealthy, retired and very mysterious international jewel thief. Or worse.

"It is a pleasure to have you here, Miss Morgan. I've been looking forward to your company." Cardinal took Angie's hand in his own and kissed the back of it with a natural finesse that made her eyes widen in appreciation. Then he extended his hand to Flynn. "Mr. Sangrey? We weren't expecting you but please feel welcomed."

Flynn accepted the handshake easily. "Thank you. Angie was kind enough to invite me along. I'm glad you don't mind."

"Not at all, not at all. Please be seated. Haslett will be bringing drinks out in a moment."

Angie sank down onto one of the cushioned wicker chairs and turned her head to take in the exquisite view of sea and darkening sky. "Your home is absolutely magnificent, Mr. Cardinal."

"I have been fortunate over the years. And this is my reward." Cardinal smiled genially as he seated himself.

"I didn't realize there was a reward for good fortune," Angie couldn't resist saying.

"There is when a man is directly responsible for his own luck." Cardinal looked at Flynn, who had taken the chair next to Angie. "Wouldn't you agree, Mr. Sangrey?"

"Completely, Mr. Cardinal." Flynn's eyes moved appreciatively over his surroundings. "Completely."

Angie sensed quite suddenly that Flynn and Cardinal were establishing their own lines of communication, and the knowledge was vaguely alarming. She wasn't sure she liked the subtle, assessing glances that were being exchanged between the two men. Haslett appeared with a tray of drinks before she could completely analyze what was happening.

"Margaritas, sangria, or tequila and lime?" Haslett held the tray out to Angie.

She accepted one of the salt-rimmed margaritas and nodded her thanks without quite meeting Haslett's eyes. Cardinal waited until everyone had been served before he resumed the conversation.

"I am sorry your uncle could not come with you, Miss Morgan. I had been looking forward to meeting the creator of the Jake Savage series." He glanced at Flynn. "Have you read any of the books, Mr. Sangrey?"

Flynn smiled. "Angie was just asking me the same thing. I told her I had read one or two."

"They are very good from a technical point of view, aren't they?"

"Quite accurate," Flynn agreed. He flicked a quick, amused glance at Angie.

"I have enjoyed my correspondence with Julian Torres enormously," Cardinal continued. "He seems to be a man who understands the important things in life. So few men do these days."

Angie sipped her drink. "He's very grateful to you for agreeing to sell the Torres Dagger."

"I would never have agreed to do so except to someone like your uncle who had a prior claim on the dagger. It is a fine piece of steel. Beautifully worked. I'm glad it will be going back into the family that originally owned it. As we grow older, Miss Morgan, such things as family traditions become increasingly important.''

Flynn tasted the raw tequila he had accepted from Haslett. ''Angie isn't interested in family traditions. She believes in living in the present.''

''There is no way to avoid living in the present,'' Cardinal said. ''But the present has so much more meaning when the past is understood and appreciated, don't you think?''

''Of course the past is important.'' Sitting there under the scrutiny of the two men, Angie felt as if she had to defend herself. ''But it should never be allowed to dominate the present or influence decisions that must be made for the future. It also shouldn't be given undue importance. Traditions are all very well and good, but to do something simply for the sake of tradition is meaningless. The Torres Dagger is, according to Julian, very interesting and a fine example of craftsmanship. But to think that the reason two families have practically died out was because the dagger was lost a couple of generations back is ridiculous.''

''Is that how your uncle feels? I would not have thought of Julian Torres as a superstitious man.'' Cardinal steepled his fingers and regarded Angie with an inquiring gaze.

She flushed, aware that she'd overstated the case. ''Naturally Julian doesn't attribute any magic to the dagger. But I think it's become symbolic to him. He's the last male of our line and it somehow represents the whole history of the family.''

"It represents the history of another family, too," Flynn pointed out softly. "According to the story, Maria Isabel Torres brought that dagger with her when she married the neighboring landholder. It seems to me that the descendants of her children have more claim to the dagger than Julian Torres does."

Angie shrugged. "Julian doesn't think there are any descendants left."

Cardinal considered the issue. "Fascinating. Yet you are not overly interested, Miss Morgan."

Angie smiled. "I think the dagger's symbolic meaning has become far too important to Julian. He's thought of nothing else for weeks now, ever since you agreed to sell. He was very disappointed when he came down with the flu and was forced to send me in his place."

"As I said, family traditions often become more important to us as we grow older." Cardinal sipped his drink. "Those of us who reach a certain age and realize that the family will not live on after us find it…disturbing." His blue eyes became curiously shadowed.

Flynn leaned forward, his elbows on his knees, his drink cradled between his palms. "Traditions are important in other ways, too, not just for nostalgic reasons. Angie says there's no magic in the dagger, but maybe there is."

Cardinal gave him an interested glance. "In what sense, Mr. Sangrey?"

"For two families that dagger represents history and power. It may be only a symbol, but symbols are important. Wars and revolutions have been fought over symbolic objects. Legends grow up around such objects for a reason. From what Angie tells me, there's no denying the fact that both families associated with the Torres Dagger began to die out after the thing was sold off back in the twenties. Maybe something important was lost when the dagger disappeared.''

''Such as?'' Angie challenged.

''Such as a unifying focus, a sense of tradition, a commitment to keeping the families strong. Who knows? All I'm saying is that you shouldn't discount the power of that dagger.''

Angie sighed. ''Well, it will make Julian very happy to have it back and for that reason alone, it's worth your price, Mr. Cardinal.''

The older man smiled approvingly. ''You appear to be quite loyal to your uncle, Miss Morgan. Loyalty is a valuable commodity in this day and age. In any day and age, for that matter. Don't you agree, Mr. Sangrey?''

Flynn looked at Angie, his expression unreadable. ''Loyalty is more than merely a valuable commodity, Mr. Cardinal. It's priceless.''

''You are obviously a man who has learned that lesson well.'' Cardinal rose to his feet and extended his arm to Angie. ''If you will accompany me, I will show you my collection. The dagger is waiting to be claimed.''

Angie accepted his arm, aware that Flynn was following close behind. Cardinal led the way back into the villa and on into a windowless room that had been paneled in teak. When he opened the door to reveal the collection of antique weapons, Angie thought she heard a soft exclamation from Flynn. Apparently Cardinal did, too, because he dropped Angie's arm and turned to watch his other guest with an amused and understanding eye.

"What do you think, Mr. Sangrey?"

Flynn's gaze moved from the pike hung on one wall to a handsomely worked bowie knife housed in a glass case. "Very impressive." He walked over to another case and studied a sword that lay on black silk. The pommel was done in deeply etched silver.

"From Toledo," Cardinal murmured.

"Yes." Flynn continued to gaze at the weapon. "Eighteenth century?"

"Probably earlier."

Angie watched Flynn move on to a wall that was hung with wicked-looking two-edged swords. She remembered her own comment the previous evening when she had wondered aloud how much Flynn would have in common with Cardinal.

"My collection of rapiers is still growing," Cardinal remarked as he walked over to stand beside Flynn. He reached up, took one off the wall and examined it lovingly for a moment. Then he handed it to Flynn. "French. Sixteen hundreds."

Angie moved uneasily. The roomful of weapons was reawakening the nervousness that Alexander Cardinal had partially put to rest with his gracious hospitality. It wasn't just the sight of the instruments of war that was disturbing, it was the deep fascination they clearly held for Flynn and Cardinal. She began to hope Haslett would show up soon to announce dinner.

"Ah, Miss Morgan, are we boring you?" Cardinal looked politely concerned.

"No, of course not," she assured him quickly, not wanting to seem rude. Flynn didn't look up from the rapier he was holding. "It's quite an interesting collection," she added, aware that the words sounded weak.

Cardinal smiled understandingly. "Perhaps you would find the object of your quest more interesting." He moved soundlessly across the room to pick up a closed, black leather case. With a small bow he handed it to Angie. "The Torres Dagger."

Angie glanced down at the obviously new case and then back up to find Flynn watching her intently. Wordlessly she unfastened the catch.

The case was lined with black velvet. The dagger lay sheathed in very old leather, its handle gleaming faintly with the semiprecious stones that had been set in it. The weapon wasn't very large, Angie thought. The whole thing, handle and blade, was about a foot long. Slim, sleek, and deadly. Holding the case in one hand, she touched the handle of the dagger with her free fingers. For a few seconds she was unable to look away from the contents of the case. Without stopping to think, she closed her hand tightly around the handle and lifted the sheathed blade out of the case.

The odd sensation of possessiveness was startling. She had never seen the Torres Dagger before in her life. And she certainly didn't believe all that much about its importance to either the Torres or Challoner family.

So why did she suddenly feel as if the dagger belonged to her?

Three

The launch and its near-silent pilot delivered Angie and Flynn to the hotel dock three hours later. The boat roared off into the night as its two passengers started up the steps toward the resort. Angie didn't bother to wave goodbye.

"It seems to me, Mr. Cardinal could afford a more pleasant staff." Angie clutched the dagger case under her arm as Flynn guided her back toward the lights of the lobby. She could hear the sounds of the lounge combo drifting out over the hotel gardens.

"I have a hunch Cardinal has exactly the sort of staff he wants," Flynn said blandly. "In fact, I'd say Mr. Cardinal gets most of what he wants in life."

"He probably makes it a 'Cardinal rule.'"

"I have the feeling that maybe he hasn't got one thing, though."

"A family?" Angie hazarded.

"Yeah."

"What do you suppose his background really is, Flynn?"

"There are some people in this world you don't ask that question about."

People such as you? Angie wanted to ask but didn't. She felt a strange wistfulness settle on her as she remembered that she would be leaving Mexico the next day.

"Let's get a nightcap in the lounge."

"All right." She slanted him a smile. "Thanks for coming with me tonight, Flynn."

"No problem."

"I guess I was worrying for no reason."

"Looks like it."

"You still haven't told me how much you're charging," she ventured tentatively.

His fingers closed rather tightly around her elbow. The set of his face was grim. "You don't really think I'm going to bill you for tonight's services, do you?"

"Well, we did have an agreement. I want to keep up my end of the deal."

"Shut up, Angie."

Humor bubbled up inside her. "You're not supposed to talk to your employer that way. Didn't you notice how respectful Cardinal's employees were to him?"

"Yes," he agreed. "But since I'm not going to

charge you for tonight, you're not my employer. Just a lady who's a little close to stepping out of line.'' He hustled her into the lounge and found a vacant table in the corner. After ordering two coffee liqueurs he leaned forward to study her face above the flickering glow of the candle. His eyes were dark and penetrating. ''What are you going to do with the dagger tonight?''

Angie touched the leather case lying on the table. ''Put it in the hotel safe, I think.'' She paused. ''It's beautiful, isn't it?''

''How would I know? You've hardly let me get near it.'' There was an edge to the words.

Angie chuckled. ''Sorry.'' She opened the case for him. The candlelight danced on the gems in the dagger's handle. ''Maria Isabel must have meant business on her wedding night. This is no toy.''

Flynn sat staring silently at the dagger for a long moment. ''No,'' he said at last. ''It's no toy.'' He touched the handle briefly and then withdrew his hands, folding his arms on the table. ''I think Maria Isabel had some very serious intentions toward her new husband. I can imagine what he must have thought when she pulled this beauty out of her robe.''

''She was a very brave woman.''

''Try arrogant, headstrong and reckless,'' Flynn suggested dryly.

''She was brave! It took courage to plan to defend herself on her wedding night.'' More than ever she felt compelled to champion the unknown Maria Isabel.

"You sound awfully sympathetic all of a sudden. I thought you considered this whole business a nuisance."

Angie drummed her fingertips on the table, wondering why she was bothering to argue Maria Isabel's side of the story. "I don't know. Something about seeing the dagger made me realize just how angry and frightened she must have been to take it with her that night."

"Would you have taken it with you on your wedding night?"

The soft question sent a ripple of tension through Angie. She reached out abruptly and closed the leather case. "We'll never know, will we?" She forced a smile. "Times have changed. These days, women in the States aren't often used as a means of sealing alliances between families. At least not at my social level."

She'd meant it as a joke, but to her astonishment Flynn took the comment seriously. His mouth tightened. "No, they marry for other reasons, don't they? For money or because a few hours of passion have convinced them they're in love. Sometimes they get married because all their friends are getting married. And sometimes they get married because they're bored and lonely and afraid of getting old."

"For a man who apparently doesn't spend a lot of time in the States these days, you seem to have some rather well-developed sociological theories," Angie snapped, annoyed.

"The only point I'm trying to make is that a marriage made for the sake of forming a family alliance is as good a reason as any other. Better reason than most.'' The hardness left Flynn's face briefly as his mouth crooked humorously. ''At some point during her wedding night, Maria Isabel must have come to the same conclusion. After all, you know she didn't use the dagger.''

Angie bit back a thoroughly disgusted retort. ''Obviously you have your world view and I have mine,'' she said smoothly instead.

''Who are you going to marry, Angie? And why?''

''I have absolutely no idea *who* I'll marry, but the reason will be because I've fallen madly, passionately, wildly in love,'' she stated with grand conviction. ''I won't give a damn about the history of his family or its future fortunes.''

''Maria Isabel probably said something along those lines herself when her father told her he'd made the deal with the neighbor. Apparently her father was wise enough to ignore the dramatics.''

Angie refused to let him goad her further. ''You seem very interested in the tale of Maria Isabel and the two families connected with this dagger. Have you got much family of your own, Flynn?''

He shook his head, his expression suddenly remote. ''Not anymore.''

Instantly Angie felt contrite. She was obviously treading on forbidden ground now. ''I'm sorry, Flynn. I didn't mean to pry.''

He hesitated and then said, ''It's all right. Your question is logical under the circumstances. I've been on my own for quite a while. A long time ago

I was eighteen years old and I did what a lot of other kids do at eighteen. I enlisted. One thing led to another. After I got out of the military there were other jobs.'' He paused, as if memories were moving in his dark eyes. ''Every year it seemed I found myself farther and farther away from anyplace I could call home.''

''And now?'' she asked softly.

''And now I'm pushing forty and realizing I'm still a long way from home.'' Flynn smiled abruptly. ''What time do you leave tomorrow, Angie?''

She accepted the change of topic, knowing he had already said more than he had intended. ''Not until the afternoon. My plane leaves at 3:45. The airport outside of Cancun is about an hour's drive from here. There's a shuttle bus that leaves the hotel at 2:00.'' Angie fell silent, realizing that she would never see this enigmatic man again after tomorrow. It was an odd sensation, far more depressing than it should have been.

''By tomorrow evening you'll be back in California.'' Flynn looked down at his glass of liqueur.

''Los Angeles. I'll spend the night there in an airport hotel and go on up the coast to Julian's home the next day.'' Angie found herself staring down at her own after-dinner drink. Quite suddenly there didn't seem to be a great deal more to say. Silence descended on the little table in the corner of the lounge.

''I don't suppose,'' Flynn finally said, ''that you'd be interested in some company on the trip home?''

Angie's head came up abruptly, her eyes full of questions. Flynn was watching her with more than his customary intensity. "Company?" Her mouth felt dry.

He spoke carefully, clearly feeling his way. "It's been a while since I was in California."

She licked her lips. "You're on vacation."

"True." He lifted his glass and drank from it.

"Do you…do you have the time to spare?"

"I have no, uh, pressing engagements," he murmured dryly. Flynn lowered his glass. "You haven't answered the question. Would you want my company?"

Angie took a deep breath. "I would very much enjoy having your company on the way home." She felt suddenly light-headed. The sense of depression that had been gathering around her dissipated. He was coming home with her.

They sat looking at each other for long moments, and then Flynn broke the silent tension to glance at the black metal watch on his wrist. "It's late."

"Yes, I suppose it is."

"I'd better get you up to your room. We can get up early and go swimming before breakfast."

"That sounds wonderful." She couldn't think of anything else to say.

She wasn't the only one finding herself short of conversation all of a sudden, Flynn thought. He couldn't find a great deal to say, either, now that he'd accomplished his goal. The realization that it was all working out beautifully left him with an unexpected feeling of ambivalence. Not knowing what else to do, he got to his feet and waited for Angie to pick up the dagger case. Silently he guided her out of the lounge.

As they walked into the lobby he decided he had nothing to lose by playing a long sheet. ''I could keep the dagger in my room tonight if you like.''

Angie's fingers tightened around the case. ''That's all right. The hotel safe is probably the best place for it.'' She smiled brightly. ''I don't want you to feel responsible for it.''

Flynn nodded, accepting the inevitable. He waited patiently at the front desk while Angie talked to the bilingual clerk. She spoke in English. A few minutes later, after seeing the dagger safely locked away, Flynn led Angie toward the elevator.

''Don't you speak Spanish?''

''Just a little California pidgin, why?''

''Well, with your family history and all, I guess I assumed you might have learned Spanish somewhere along the line.''

She smiled. ''I've told you before, I'm not exactly mesmerized by my past. Your Spanish is excellent, I've noticed.''

He shrugged and said nothing.

''Thanks again for going with me to Cardinal's this evening,'' Angie said at her door.

Flynn glanced down at her fingertips, which she'd impulsively placed on his sleeve. ''Thanks for asking me along.'' He saw the warmth in her eyes and felt the answering wave of urgency that pulsed through his own body. She seemed to trust him now. And she seemed to want him. It might be safe to let

the physical attraction that flared between them take
its course.

He raised his hand to let his fingers rest against
the side of her throat. He could feel the excitement
in her. It fueled his own desire as nothing else could
have done. Flynn leaned forward and kissed her
slowly, savoring the willing response he received.
His fingers tightened fractionally on her throat, and
his thumb moved luxuriously just under the line of
her jaw. She was so soft and delicate, he thought,
but with a woman's strength.

He'd seen her swimming energetically, watched
her walking along the beach with a long, healthy
stride. She wasn't at all fragile, and yet she made
him think of fragile things. Things that should be
protected.

A door opened at the end of the hall and reluctantly Flynn raised his head. Angie looked up at him
with a tentative appeal. She was still uncertain of
how far this should go tonight. But if he pushed a
little, Flynn was sure he could push her straight into
bed.

But there was so much else to consider. So much
at stake. It would be better to wait a while longer,
he knew. Better to let her think that he wasn't at all
the type to push.

The ironic part was that it had been years since
he'd felt so much like pushing a woman. God, how
he wanted her tonight. He had to remember that
there was a lot more involved here than one night
in bed. He was no boy. He could control himself
and his hormones. It would be so much more effec-

tive to keep her dangling; to ignite the flames in her and then let them blaze for a while. So much more useful. He'd learned his lesson last night. It was crucial to be the one who set the pace and called the moves.

"Good night, Angie," he whispered huskily. He stepped back, pretending to be oblivious to the flicker of disappointment in her expression. She recovered quickly with a smile.

"Good night, Flynn." She turned the key in the lock and then she was gone.

Flynn went on up to his own room with the distinct impression that he'd been ridiculously overcautious. The heavy, unsatisfied ache in his lower body reinforced that thought for the next hour.

Implementing sound strategy could be hard on a man.

Angie came awake a few hours later with the terrifying knowledge that something was very, very wrong.

The illogical fear kept her breathlessly still in the center of the wide bed. Some primitive survival instinct warned her not to open her eyes. Adrenaline surged through her veins and she thought she could hear the thudding beat of her own heart.

Perhaps she'd awakened on the heels of some nightmare, she thought, striving to understand her fear. But she couldn't remember any scenes of horror. It hadn't been a dream that had awakened her, it had been a small, almost insignificant sound.

There was someone in her room.

She'd heard the words "paralyzed with fright," but she'd never understood them until this moment. The sound came again; a faint, gliding noise such as a shoe might make on thick carpeting.

Frantically Angie strove to still the mindless fear that was threatening to take full control of her body. She had two options, she told herself. She could scream for help or keep utterly still and allow the intruder to believe she was asleep. Somewhere she had read that the latter was the safer course. If whoever was in the room was intent on robbery, he would be looking for her purse. As soon as he found it, he would be gone.

If she screamed she risked causing the thief to panic and do something crazy such as use a gun or a knife to silence her.

Where was he in the room? Lying motionless Angie struggled to control her breathing. It seemed far too loud in her own ears. She was wringing wet with fear.

She was on her side facing the balcony. The faint gliding noise came again from the vicinity of the nightstand. He must be searching the drawers. Please let him find the purse quickly.

Angie thought she detected soft sounds near the chair where she had left her shoulder bag. *There. It's right there in front of you. Grab it. Take it and leave. Get out of here.*

What was the matter with the idiot? Couldn't he see the yellow leather bag just sitting there on the chair? She had the drapes open, and the room was not completely dark. Why didn't he take the damn purse?

The whisper of sound came again, this time from near the foot of the bed. A new fear assailed her. If the intruder had more than theft on his mind, she would have no choice but to start screaming and risk the knife or the gun. Her hand clenched silently into a fist, her nails digging into her palm.

Then, without any further warning, the door to her room opened and closed in near silence. She was alone.

The knowledge that the intruder had gone left Angie weak with an almost physically painful sense of relief. For a long moment she simply lay on her side, inhaling deeply in an attempt to steady her nerves. Her legs were trembling beneath the sheet.

She opened her eyes and stared out at the starlit balcony. The ocean gleamed in the distance as the moon painted a broad swath of silver across its surface. She wanted comfort and warmth and safety.

She wanted the feel of Flynn's strong arms around her. She wanted his protection.

Angie kicked off the sheet with a burst of energy that surprised her. She darted to the closet, yanked down her terry-cloth swim robe and belted it around her waist. Then she grabbed her room key and let herself out into the hall.

There was no sign of anyone in the corridor. Not bothering with the elevator, she headed for the stairwell and dashed up the two flights to the floor where Flynn's room was located. Panting, she halted outside the door and rapped sharply.

When it opened a moment later Angie didn't hesitate. She hurled herself into Flynn's arms.

"Angie! What the hell…?" He held her close.

"There was someone in my room. A thief. He was prowling around my room, Flynn." The words came out in short gasps. "I've never been so scared in my life. I was sure I'd locked the door. I don't understand how—" She broke off, recovered her breath and tried again. "As soon as he left I ran up here. He must have been after my purse, but he didn't take it. I guess he couldn't see it. Oh, my God, I was terrified!"

"Angie! Angie, honey, calm down. Tell me exactly what happened." Flynn's hands closed around her upper arms and he shook her gently. "Are you sure someone was in your room?"

She nodded her head sharply. "Hell, yes. I could hear him. A sort of gliding sound on the carpet. Flynn, nothing like this has ever happened to me before in my life. It's so frightening." With an effort she gathered herself together. Then she tried a shaky smile. "It's okay, I'm not going to flip out on you."

Flynn's face was hard and grim, his dark eyes glittering with controlled tension. "You're certain nothing was taken?"

"Well, no, I'm not absolutely certain. I just remember seeing my purse on the chair as I left the room a few minutes ago. I suppose he might have reached inside and taken the wallet."

"Come on."

"Where are we going?" She leaned back against the door as he released her to pick up the black shirt he'd been wearing earlier. For the first time Angie realized he was wearing only a pair of white briefs. The naked expanse of his shoulders moved sleekly as he shrugged into the shirt. He reached for a pair of jeans and quickly stepped into them. Angie glanced away from the sight of his well-muscled thighs. It was a little unsettling to encounter a nearly nude male at this hour of the night. Especially when it was a male she had gone to sleep fantasizing about a few hours earlier. She'd seen him in a swimsuit, but somehow this was different, far more intimate.

"We're going back down to your room to make certain nothing was taken. Then we're going downstairs to have a talk with the desk clerk." Flynn picked up his keys and his folded leather wallet, and then he took Angie's arm.

Obediently Angie allowed him down the stairs to her own room. She opened the door and switched on the light.

"See? There's the purse. The fool couldn't seem to see it, although it was easy enough for me to spot on my way out the door." She walked over to the chair and unfastened the catch of the shoulder bag. Her passport and billfold were still safely tucked inside.

Flynn prowled around the room, opening drawers and checking the doors that fronted the balcony. "You're sure he came and left through the hallway door?"

"Absolutely. I could hear it open and close when he left." Angie picked her bag up off the chair and sat down with it in her lap. Hands clutching the leather, she stared at Flynn as he searched the balcony. "I just don't understand how he could have missed the purse. Unless..."

Flynn walked back in from the balcony. "Unless what?"

"Unless it wasn't my purse he was after," she said starkly.

The sliding glass door closed with a vicious chunking sound. Flynn turned to face her, his gaze burning. "You're all right?"

She blinked, realizing what he was thinking. "I'm fine," she assured him. "I didn't mean that whoever it was intended rape. I meant he might be after something other than my purse. The dagger, for instance."

"The dagger!" Flynn sank onto the rumpled bed, frowning. "The only one who even knows you have it is..."

"Alexander Cardinal," she concluded for him.

"But that doesn't make any sense, Angie. He just sold it to you a few hours ago. Why would he try to get it back?"

"You saw the size of Julian's check. That dagger wasn't cheap. And Cardinal is obviously a man who goes through a lot of money. Remember the yacht? The private island? The villa? Maybe Cardinal decided he'd take Julian's money and then take back the dagger, too. The best of both worlds."

"I got the feeling that Cardinal, whatever else he might be, is a man of his word." Flynn looked thoughtful.

"A man of his word! How could you trust him?

He's obviously made a fortune and no one, including Julian, seems quite sure how. He's charming, all right, but I wouldn't trust him any farther than I could throw him. What's more, I'll bet he's got everyone in the vicinity in his pocket. It would be easy enough for him to hire someone to break into my room."

"Okay, settle down. I'm not going to argue with you about the guy. But if he's on such good terms with the hotel people, wouldn't someone have told him that you put the dagger in the safe?"

Angie shifted uneasily, thinking about it. "Who knows? Maybe he didn't bother to ask; just assumed I'd have it in my room. Flynn, I don't know what's going on, but the fact remains that the thief didn't bother with my purse, and the only other thing of value that I have is that dagger. Cardinal is too powerful in this part of Mexico. I want to leave."

"Angie, it's four in the morning."

"I don't care. I want to get the dagger and leave. Right now."

"And go where?" Flynn asked patiently.

"The airport. Maybe we can get an earlier flight."

"We?"

Angie stilled. "I thought you were coming back to California with me?"

Flynn's gaze softened. "I am. I'm just not sure it's necessary to leave right this minute."

"Flynn, you once said you believed in some forms of intuition...."

"Not feminine intuition," he drawled.

"Well, I do believe in it. And I have the strongest

feeling that we should get away from here.'' Angie looked at him pleadingly. ''Please, Flynn. I'm scared. I'm responsible for getting that dagger safely back to Julian. I don't want to take any chances. As long as we hang around the resort we're just too close to Cardinal. He's too powerful.''

''Angie, we don't even know if he's after the dagger,'' Flynn tried to say logically.

''Someone is!''

''We don't know that. The guy might have been after your purse and just missed it.'' Flynn got up and came across to her. ''Or you might have dreamed the whole thing, honey,'' he added gently. ''There's no sign of any forcible entry.''

''I did not dream it!'' She felt a rush of fury and hysteria begin to build in her. ''I thought you of all people would believe me, Flynn!''

He threaded his large fingers through her tangled hair and looked down at her for a long, considering moment. ''You're scared, aren't you?''

''Panicked.''

He gave her a half smile. ''Not quite but I can see you're getting there. Honey, I don't even know if we can get a car at this hour of the night. This is Mexico, remember? And a rather remote part of the country to boot. People down here run on their own time, even the tourist-trade people. They're not accustomed to crazy gringos who want to rent a car at four o'clock in the morning.''

''We've got to try.''

Flynn studied her a moment longer, clearly attempting to think of further arguments, but in the end he appeared to give up the effort. "Okay, Angie. I'll go downstairs and see what I can do about renting a car."

"I'll come with you."

"I had a feeling you were going to say that."

She realized with a shock that he wasn't certain yet whether he believed her tale of the intruder. His lack of faith angered her. "You don't have to humor me, Flynn. If you don't want to get involved, just go on back to your own room. I'll handle this myself." Her fingers were digging into the leather purse. Angie felt more determined than she ever had about anything in her life. "I'm not trying to force you to come with me. But I am going to get out of here tonight."

Flynn's gaze narrowed speculatively. "You know damn well I'm involved now."

"There's absolutely no need for you to go any further with this," she began defiantly. "I appreciate your help up to this point, but you certainly don't need to feel obligated to—"

"You've said enough, Angie. I'm going with you."

"Not if you're going to act patronizing or domineering, you aren't!"

He planted his palm flat against the wall behind her head and leaned over her. "You want to drive forty miles by yourself on a lonely Mexican highway at four in the morning?"

Angie flinched. The occasional tales of U.S. tourists ambushed on Mexican roads were not unknown to her. She'd researched such tales for one of Julian's books. It was relatively easy to discount those stories during the daytime, but at four in the morning they took on new meaning. But she said stubbornly, "I'd feel safer driving up the coast alone than I would staying here."

Flynn straightened away from the wall, his attitude one of resignation. "All right. I can see you're not going to be completely rational about this. Let's get going. Put some clothes on. I'm not taking you down to the front desk dressed like that."

She stood up slowly. "You don't believe me, do you?"

"I believe something scared the hell out of you tonight. But in all honesty I can't see any sign of someone having been in your room. And from what you've told me, you didn't actually see anyone, either. You just think you heard him."

Angie gritted her teeth and turned to pull a pair of jeans and a red cotton-knit pullover out of the closet. Without a word she headed toward the bathroom to change.

Ten minutes later Flynn had roused the sleeping desk clerk and explained the need to rent a car. The clerk rubbed his eyes, yawned widely and politely explained that renting a car was quite impossible at this hour of the night.

"The rental agency will not be open until nine this morning, *señor.* Surely you can understand that." The clerk smiled ingratiatingly, trying hard to be polite to the crazy *norteamericanos.* His uncle had warned him when he'd hired him that a night clerk's job was not always easy. Tourists were a strange bunch.

Flynn pulled out his wallet and peeled off several large bills. He put them down on the counter in front of the clerk. "I am prepared to pay someone for the inconvenience of renting us a car. Could you please telephone whoever is responsible for running the rental agency here in the hotel and ask if he's interested in being compensated for the extra trouble?"

The clerk looked down at the bills. Tourists were not only very strange, they were willing to pay dearly for the oddest things. Women, cigarettes made from a local product that, thanks to the vagaries of bureaucrats, could not be marketed legally; such things he could understand a man being willing to waste money on. But a rental car at four o'clock in the morning? It made no sense.

But a night desk clerk learned to be sophisticated about such matters. The clerk smiled brilliantly and put two fingers on one of the bills. "There is no way a car can be rented at this hour, but there is a possible alternative. Where is it you wish to travel, *señor?*"

Flynn kept his hand firmly on the money. "Cancun."

Angie, standing behind him, waited anxiously as the clerk appeared to give considerable thought to the matter. With every passing moment she felt the need to be on her way with the dagger.

"Cancun." The clerk nodded. "A long trip by car but not so long by boat. My cousin, Ramon, has a very fast boat, *señor.* He uses it to pull the tourists on water skis. I think that I might be able to convince him to take you to Cancun."

"He'd take us down the coast in the darkness?" Flynn looked distinctly skeptical.

The clerk shrugged. "It is nearly four-thirty. In another half hour it will be dawn. Besides, Ramon has lived here all his life. He knows the coastline as well as he knows the faces of his six children."

Flynn turned back to Angie. "Are you sure you don't want to wait until the rental agency opens?"

She didn't hesitate. "I'm sure."

He studied her determined expression and gave in to the inevitable. Nothing he said was going to change her mind, he realized. "Okay. Call Cousin Ramon," Flynn said to the clerk.

The man's hand closed around the cash lying on the desk. Then, beaming, he disappeared into an office. Flynn wondered idly how much the clerk would tell his cousin he'd received from the crazy *norte-americano*. He figured Ramon would be lucky to see half the bribe.

The clerk had been right. By the time Angie and Flynn had packed, checked out of the hotel and found a cheery-looking Ramon waiting at the dock, there was a faint glow lightening the sky. The sun would be rising soon. Flynn was grateful for small favors. He hadn't been looking forward to making this little jaunt in total darkness.

"Cancun?" Ramon repeated easily when Flynn told him the destination. "No sweat." He grinned proudly at his fine English.

"That's just terrific, Ramon," Flynn said dryly as

he settled himself down beside Angie. "Absolutely terrific. Let's get going." He glanced at Angie's tense face as Ramon pulled the boat away from the dock. The dagger case was resting on her lap. She didn't seem willing to trust it to the small bag that rested at her feet. When he saw the anxiety in her eyes, some of his irritation lessened. She was genuinely frightened. "Feeling better now that we're on our way?"

She nodded briefly. "Yes. Thank you for arranging everything, Flynn. I will see that you're compensated for the money you had to give the desk clerk."

"Angie, do me a favor. If you're going to insist on maintaining that insulted-employer-dealing-with-untrusting-employee attitude, keep your mouth shut, okay? I'm not in the mood for placating you right now. I've got other things on my mind."

She glared at him. "Such as?"

"I'll think of something."

A few minutes later Flynn stopped wondering what else to think about. Something rather crucial came to mind as he glanced back over his shoulder at the lights of the resort.

"Hell."

The roar of the boat's engine masked the soft oath, but Angie must have seen his expression. She stared at his profile for a few seconds and then leaned toward him.

"What's wrong?" She held her whipping hair out of her eyes.

"I'm not sure yet." He spoke into her ear so that

she could hear him above the noise of the boat and the wind. "But I think Cousin Ramon was wrong. I'm afraid we have got something to sweat about."

Angie's eyes widened in startled concern. "What are you talking about?"

But Flynn was on his feet, heading toward the front of the speeding craft, where Ramon stood at the wheel. He leaned down to tap the pilot on his shoulder.

"*Señor?*" Ramon glanced up, his face a mask of polite inquiry.

"What the hell do you think you're doing?" Flynn said, raising his voice above the engine roar. "You've been hired to take us down the coast. I didn't pay you for a sightseeing trip of the bay."

"I am very sorry, *señor*, but someone else has paid me for taking you sightseeing. And I'm also sorry to report he paid a great deal more than you did for your run to Cancun. So what can I do? I have six children to feed. We go sightseeing instead of down the coast."

Cousin Ramon raised his hand and revealed the ugly .25-caliber Star semiautomatic he had clutched in his fist.

Four

Angie couldn't hear the verbal exchange between Cousin Ramon and Flynn; the roar of the outboard blanked out the words. But moonlight glinted on the gun in Ramon's hand when he raised his arm. She froze in her seat.

She saw Flynn glance almost casually down at the weapon. In the chancy light she thought he looked more wryly disgusted than alarmed. It occurred to her that this probably wasn't the first time he had encountered a man with a gun.

He said something to the Mexican, something Ramon appeared to consider seriously for a moment. Angie guessed Flynn was following local custom and offering a bribe. It was obvious Ramon was torn, but he finally shook his head with grave regret. Evidently whoever was paying him to do this was someone he didn't want to risk offending, Angie decided. Alexander Cardinal was a local employer, after all. The gringos could only offer a one-time arrangement and then they would be gone. Mr. Cardinal undoubtedly offered the opportunity of future employment. And Cousin Ramon had all those kids to support.

Angie was aware of the trickle of dampness running down her arm. The early morning air was balmy, even a bit on the cool side, but she was perspiring as if it were already high noon. The odd part was that she didn't feel warm. She felt distinctly chilled. She sat very still, the box holding the dagger clutched on her lap.

Flynn was still talking to Ramon. Trying to bargain, perhaps. The outboard continued to roar at high speed as Ramon kept one hand casually on the wheel. Unsteadily Angie got to her feet. Instantly the eyes of both men flicked to the back of the boat. Ramon's gaze only wavered for a second, but when he saw Angie he hissed something to Flynn.

"Stay where you are, Angie." Flynn waved her back to her seat with a short, chopping movement of his hand.

She ignored him, making her way to the midpoint of the small craft. Hanging on to the dagger box, she maintained her balance with her free hand by clinging to the side of the boat.

"What does he want?" She was close enough to hear the voices of the two men now.

It was Ramon who answered in English. "Very sorry, *señorita.* But I have been told to take you to the island."

"Cardinal's island?"

Flynn shot her another glance. "Sit down, Angie."

She looked at him and then held up the dagger box. "He wants this. I knew it. He's going to try to steal it back."

Ramon glanced skeptically at the box, but his gun hand didn't waver. "I do not know why I am taking you to the island. I only do what I am told."

"This is why you're taking us to Cardinal's island. Cardinal wants this dagger back." Angrily Angie flipped open the lid of the box. She saw Ramon tense at the abrupt movement.

Then his curiosity got the better of him. He stared at the object lying on the black velvet. Caught by the moonlight, the gems in the dagger's handle gleamed richly. The steel picked up the faint yellow cast of the light and for an instant a man could have been forgiven for thinking that the object was made of gold and diamonds.

"I won't let him have it," Angie went on. She held the box out over the side of the boat. "I'll drop it into the ocean before I hand it back to Señor Cardinal."

"*Señorita!*" Ramon's eyes widened in alarm as he read the intent on her face. She stood there with the dagger box held precariously out over the foaming water. If he shot her now, the dagger would fall straight into the sea. Ramon panicked. "Tell her to stop!" he roared at Flynn.

"The lady's got a mind of her own." Flynn stood casually, one hand idly bracing himself on the top of the windshield.

"Tell her to stop or I will kill you!"

Angie's fingers tightened on the box, but she didn't bring it back to safety. Her hair whipped savagely around her face as she glared at the Mexican. "Pull that trigger, Ramon, and this thing goes into the water. Señor Cardinal will be furious, won't he?"

Ramon swore violently in Spanish, his face suddenly contorting with rage. Wildly he swung the gun away from Flynn, his intent clear.

But Flynn was in motion before the weapon could be trained on Angie. His hand came away from the windshield in a movement that resembled a striking snake. The quick, savage blow sliced into Ramon's wrist. Even as Ramon's howl of pain and rage began, Flynn was driving his other fist into the man's jaw.

A shot crashed through the night and then the semiautomatic flew into the air as Ramon sagged backward against the wheel. The boat swung crazily as his weight replaced the guidance of his hand.

"Flynn! The boat!" Hastily Angie snatched the dagger back to safety. She staggered, trying to catch her balance as the craft swerved abruptly.

Flynn yanked the half-conscious, groaning Ramon away from the wheel and tossed him down into the seat. Then he reached out to take control of the boat. A moment later the world steadied again. Flynn cut the engine.

Angie sat down abruptly as the boat came to a gliding halt in the water. It bobbed gently on the waves as Flynn released the wheel to concentrate on Ramon.

"Are you all right?"

Angie knew the harsh question was directed at her, not at the man sprawling on the seat. She huddled into herself, trying to stop shaking. Her body seemed to be going first hot and then cold. "Yes," she gasped. "Yes, I'm fine."

"Good. Then put down that damn dagger and come take the wheel."

It took a surprising amount of effort to unlock her fingers from the box, Angie discovered. But she managed it, setting the object carefully down on the rear seat. Uncertainly she got to her feet.

"You saved us, Flynn."

"No, Angie, I think I'll let you have full credit for this idiotic situation."

"What are we going to do with him?" She scrambled over Ramon's feet to get to the wheel.

"Dump him."

Her eyes widened in shock. "Overboard?"

"That would be the simplest answer. But I guess we can afford to be generous. We'll head back toward shore and leave him on the beach somewhere." Flynn was rapidly going through Ramon's pockets.

"What are you looking for?"

"I'd like to know who hired him."

"It's obvious who hired him. That horrible Alexander Cardinal!"

"Maybe. Maybe not." Flynn produced a wicked-looking switchblade knife, a wad of Mexican currency and some loose change from one pocket. The next yielded a supply of gum wrappers and a half stick of gum. There was nothing else to be found.

"Looks like he's not carrying a nice, neat, notarized contract signed by Cardinal," Angie observed. "But you can't have any real doubts about who hired him, Flynn. It must have been Cardinal."

"It does look suspiciously like that, doesn't it?" Flynn finished his task and then began rummaging around in one of the boat's storage compartments.

"Now what?" Angie watched him intently.

"I need something to tie his hands with. Ah, here we go. Fishing line. That should do the trick."

A few minutes later Cousin Ramon lay securely bound in the back of the boat. He groaned occasionally but other than that made no real effort to communicate. Flynn took the wheel, switched on the engine and headed toward shore. They were a couple of miles up the coast, out of sight of the resort.

"How did you know he was going to kidnap us?" Angie sat up front, peering through the windshield as dawn warmed the horizon.

"It was no great burst of cunning logic. I simply realized, finally, that the lights of the resort were at our back as we left the dock and they didn't shift. They stayed in the same position behind us as they did the night we were taken to Cardinal's island. They should have altered position as we turned toward Cancun. I guess good old Cousin Ramon figured that in the darkness we might not notice until it was too late."

"That was very quick of you, Flynn," Angie said admiringly.

He cocked an eyebrow, slanting her an odd glance. "Not as quick as you were when you thought of distracting him by threatening to drop the dagger overboard."

She grinned suddenly. "We're a pretty good team, aren't we? Maybe Julian will want to interview us for a scene in one of his books."

"Somehow I think this might be a little tame by his standards."

"Oh, I don't know. It's definitely got possibilities. After we drop Ramon off, are we going to use the boat to go on to Cancun?"

"That's the general idea. Unless I get struck by something more brilliant in the meantime."

But Flynn was not struck by anything more brilliant. He guided the outboard carefully into a small cove, waded ashore with a sluggish, complaining Ramon and left his burden on the beach.

"Nice of you to leave him above the high-tide mark," Angie murmured as Flynn climbed, dripping, back into the boat.

"I thought so. Okay, let's get this crazy show on the road."

"What'll we do with Cousin Ramon's boat?"

"We'll beach it somewhere outside of town and walk the rest of the way."

"You think of everything, Flynn."

"There was a time not too long ago when I would have modestly agreed with you. I've since changed my mind." The wind caught his short, dark hair, ruffling it as he guided the boat out of the cove. "What a night. You sure do know how to show a guy a good time. I'm going to be exhausted by the time we reach L.A.''

Angie, who was feeling surprisingly exhilarated by the adrenaline that was still churning in her bloodstream, felt as if she could stay awake forever. She smiled to herself as she cradled the dagger box in her lap.

"Thanks, Flynn. I really mean it. I think you probably saved my life tonight. I don't even want to think about how it all would have ended if you hadn't gotten involved.'' Her gratitude was clear in her eyes.

Flynn looked down at her, aware once again of how much those beautiful eyes reminded him of the color of a peacock's tail. She really was grateful, he realized. He was startled at how pleased that made him feel. It must be his ego at work. Then he remembered his violent surge of rage and fear as he'd watched Ramon swing the gun toward her earlier. For an instant he felt that rage and fear again as he thought of her facing that gun alone.

What followed the episode on the boat constituted what Angie came to think of as the longest day of her entire life. The trip to Los Angeles seemed to take forever. There were delays while she and Flynn waited for a plane in Cancun and again in Mexico City. The time spent sitting nervously in airports kept Angie fretting constantly. Flynn had catnapped and thumbed through Spanish-language magazines, but Angie hadn't been able to relax. Even though she knew that they were undoubtedly far out of reach of Alexander Cardinal by the time they changed planes in Mexico City, she didn't really begin to calm down until their U.S. jet flew over the border.

She would have held on to the dagger case the entire distance, never letting it out of her sight, if Flynn hadn't put his foot down.

"Try to get on board clutching that thing to your bosom and we're both going to spend some time explaining ourselves to the authorities. Mexico might be a little more lax about airport security regulations than the States, but I'd just as soon not take any chances. Pack the dagger into your suitcase, Angie."

Reluctantly Angie agreed. She didn't always approve of Flynn's somewhat authoritarian manner, but by now she trusted him implicitly. She still shuddered to think of what would have happened to her at the resort if she hadn't met Flynn Sangrey.

"I suppose you're right," she responded, unlocking her suitcase, "but if they lose our luggage I'm going to hold you responsible."

He'd grinned fleetingly. "I'd rather search for lost luggage than try to find you in a Mexican jail. Stay here while I check the tickets."

They'd eaten on board the flight from Mexico City to Los Angeles, but Angie couldn't even remember what she'd had. She and Flynn had been wide awake and on the move since nearly four in the morning. They'd had to take whatever flights they could get, and after the seemingly endless delays, darkness had fallen by the time Los Angeles sprawled below the plane.

"I never thought I'd by happy to see L.A." Angie glanced through the window at the maze of freeways and the endless sea of lights.

Flynn gave her a wry glance. "Goes to show you can learn to appreciate anything under the right circumstances. What now, Angie? You look exhausted."

"I am. And you don't look so perky yourself. Might as well get a hotel room for the night. We're safe now." She stifled a small yawn. "We can drive up the coast in the morning. My car's in the airport garage." She turned to him impulsively, her fingertips on his sleeve. "Thanks for coming this far with me, Flynn. Do you…do you still want to go on up the coast and meet Uncle Julian?"

"After all this you think I'm going to stop in L.A.? Not a chance." He covered her hand on his sleeve, his strong fingers enclosing hers completely.

Angie smiled tremulously. She suddenly wished she didn't look so weary and travel worn. But the truth was she felt exhausted, and she knew it probably showed. While waiting for the plane in Mexico City she had tried to brush her hair back into its normal coil but tendrils had again straggled free. The jeans and pullover she had put on in the early morning hours seemed to hang limply on her now, and she wasn't altogether certain her twenty-four-hour deodorant was living up to its advertising.

Flynn didn't look radically different than he had

when they'd started out on the ill-fated trip with Cousin Ramon. His dark cotton shirt was wrinkled, but somehow on him it looked appropriate that way. Like something out of the catalog of safari gear. He looked a little travel weary but not totally exhausted. In the LAX terminal he still had plenty of strength to take charge of claiming the luggage and getting it through customs.

"Let me check the dagger," Angie said as he carried her bag out of the claim area.

Obediently he set it down and waited while she unlocked the suitcase again and examined the dagger case. "You seem to have grown rather attached to that thing," he observed dryly.

Still bent over the case, Angie smiled. "I know. I guess I feel responsible for it."

"Are you sure it doesn't amount to more than that?"

She closed the suitcase and got to her feet, pushing loose tendrils of hair back behind her ear. "Why do you say that?"

"Don't get defensive." He picked up the case again. "I was merely making a small observation."

Angie trotted a few steps in order to keep up with his long stride. She frowned as she considered his words. "You make it sound as though I'm getting obsessive about it."

"Forget it, Angie." He didn't speak again until they had finished with the formalities. Then he asked, "Where did you park the car?"

"What? Oh." Hastily she dug into her purse and

found the slip of paper on which she'd jotted down the garage space. "Here it is."

Flynn studied the number on the slip. "Okay. Let's get going."

"Where's your home, Flynn?"

"I don't have one. Not yet. I keep a furnished apartment in San Diego but it's not home."

For some reason that bothered Angie. She felt a rush of sympathy for this man who had saved her life and who had stayed loyally by her side throughout the long journey to L.A. "You'll like the hacienda," she assured him gently. "And Julian's present home is quite lovely, too. I'm sure he'll want you to stay as long as you wish."

There was a moment of silence behind her as Flynn mulled over her words. Then he said quietly, "But you don't live in his house. You live in that guest cottage you mentioned."

"I like my privacy."

"Do you need a lot of privacy?"

Angie paused to study overhead corridor signs that gave directions to the parking facilities. "As much as any other woman, I imagine. What on earth do you mean, Flynn?"

Again there was a beat of silence before he answered. "Nothing. It just occurred to me that you might need privacy because there's someone important in your life. A man. We never got around to talking about that possibility, did we, Angie?"

She felt a frisson of awareness course through her. "No," she whispered, not looking at him. "We never did. I guess people don't talk about things like that when they're vacationing at exotic foreign resorts.''

''Well?'' There was a stark edge to the question.

''No, Flynn,'' she heard herself say quietly. ''There's no one else. No one important the way you mean.'' Then, feeling that he owed her a similar response, she asked, ''What about you?''

''Like I said, I've been on my own a long time. The sort of life I've been living hasn't exactly been conducive to long-term relationships. There's no one else, Angie.''

She released the breath she hadn't realized she'd been holding and said brightly, ''The car's just up ahead.''

Flynn took charge of the driving with an easy authority that, under other circumstances, Angie might have resented. As it was, she discovered she was too tired to argue. It was a relief to let him battle the airport traffic. ''There's a big chain hotel a few blocks away,'' she murmured after another yawn. ''Why don't we stay there? I don't feel like driving any farther than absolutely necessary tonight. I can't remember when I've been this tired.''

''Suits me.'' He pulled through the turnstile and handed the garage ticket over to the attendant.

By the time they parked the car again in a hotel parking lot and started toward the huge, brightly lit lobby, Angie could hardly keep her eyes open. The shock and the adrenaline, as well as the hours of travel, had all taken their toll. She trailed along in Flynn's wake; a small, battered little rowboat sticking close to the protection of a sleek, strong battle cruiser.

Obediently she waited to one side as Flynn registered for both of them. She patted another delicate yawn as he came back to collect her and the luggage.

"You need a hot shower and a warm bed," Flynn decided. "And so do I." He took her arm, hoisted the bags and started toward the elevators.

It was so easy to go on letting him take charge, Angie told herself. And she was so very tired.

At the door to her room she started to turn around to say good-night but he just smiled crookedly and pushed open the door, following her inside.

"I got us connecting rooms," he explained.

"Oh." She wasn't quite certain what else to say to that. The truth was she had gotten so accustomed to the idea of having him close during the day that the thought of having him nearby tonight was oddly comforting. She watched him walk through her room, turning on the lights and setting down her suitcase. Then he unlocked the door between his room and hers. Key in hand, he lounged in the doorway.

"Don't forget the hot shower, Angie."

"I won't." She didn't want him to step through that door into his own room, she realized.

"I'll be within shouting distance if you need me."

"Thank you, Flynn." She smiled fleetingly. "I seem to be saying that a lot today, don't I?" She couldn't ask him to stay. It was too soon and they had been through too much today. What was the matter with her? Her fierce awareness of him was probably just a result of the events in Mexico. She was grateful to him, that was all. She wasn't in love with the man, and it was a cinch he wasn't in love with her.

And she didn't want to go to bed with a man she didn't love. She couldn't possibly want that.

So why did she want to snuggle into bed with Flynn Sangrey tonight? Why did she long for the comfort of his arms after the trials of the day?

Gratitude. That was all it was. That was all it could be and that wasn't enough. In addition, it was entirely possible that he wasn't in the least interested in making love to her. The man must be nearly as exhausted as she was. He would probably politely decline any invitation she offered. Heaven knew the embarrassment of rejection would be exceedingly awkward to live down in the morning.

Angie ran through the complete list of all the reasons why she shouldn't ask Flynn to stay with her and when she came to the end she smiled wistfully.

"Good night," she said, her eyes soft with a longing she couldn't quite conceal, not even from herself.

For a long moment Flynn studied her forlorn, frayed figure as she stood in the middle of the hotel room. Then he nodded, turned into his own room and closed the door behind him.

Angie sighed with a deep, feminine regret that seemed to well up from that alien fissure of gold that ran through her. Tonight the part of her nature that she had never quite trusted or fully understood was close to the surface. It had threatened to take control for a moment there as she had said goodnight to Flynn.

It was because she was so tired, Angie consoled herself. That was the only reason she'd come so close to surrendering to that hot-blooded streak in herself. When you were tired, all your defenses were down.

She should be grateful to Flynn for not having taken advantage of her.

That thought made her mouth curve wryly. She was already feeling enough gratitude toward Flynn Sangrey. Besides, she wasn't really certain that the small, wild streak in her nature knew anything about gratitude. She sensed it operated under its own set of rules.

The hot shower Flynn had prescribed was just what a doctor would have ordered. It released the last of the day's tension. By the time she shut off the warm spray, Angie could barely keep her eyes open. She fumbled around in her suitcase for her light cotton nightgown, checked once more to see that the dagger was where it should be and crawled wearily into bed.

Sleep claimed her just as she was wondering if it should be so hard to tell the difference between gratitude and passion. Surely gratitude didn't fill a woman with this kind of deep, abiding longing.

Angie wasn't certain just when the unfocused swirl of her dreams began to coalesce into reality.

She only knew that hours after she had gone to sleep she awoke to a sense of awareness that didn't seem to belong to either the world of sleep or the state of being alert. It was some never-never land in between, a border area between night and day that allowed for all sorts of possibilities.

Slowly she turned on her side, her eyes half-closed as she slowly studied the shadowy room. The door between her bedroom and Flynn's stood open.

The knowledge ought to have jolted her into full wakefulness. Instead Angie felt only a sense of relief, as if, finally, everything was working out the way it should. In this soft, hidden area between reality and sleep, the golden fissure within her began to glow. Unstopped by logic or a woman's natural uncertainty, it leaked its potent energy into Angie's system. The open door between the two rooms meant only one thing: Flynn was here. He had come to find her.

"Angie?" There was a low rustle of movement beside the bed. Flynn's voice was dark and deep, a little rough around the edges. The blunt tips of his fingers brushed her cheek. "If you want me to leave, I will."

Angie caught the fingers that were feathering her skin. She turned her mouth into the palm of his hand and kissed him with exquisite gentleness. "No," she whispered. "I don't want you to leave." It was the truth and in this alien borderland she was free to admit it.

"Sweet, soft Angie." Flynn lifted the light blanket and slid into the warm bed.

He was nude, Angie realized with a tingling sense of shock. What had she expected? Silk pajamas? Cautiously, but with a compelling feeling of exhilaration, she reached out to touch the muscled contours of his chest. She heard his small groan of desire and then his feet were tangling with hers.

"I've been wanting to hold you like this since the first night I met you." Flynn brought her close, one hand cradling her hips as he urged her into his own heat.

"Oh, Flynn..." She could feel the hardness of him pushing against her with unsubtle demand. Her own desire flared more fully into life, coloring the shadowy moment with gentle fire. Her body was responding to his with glorious excitement, and Angie wondered why she had ever tried to talk herself out of this union. Nothing had ever seemed so right.

She felt Flynn's strong thigh sliding up between her legs, carefully parting her own thighs so that she was open to him. His hand moved up under the hem of the cotton gown, gliding over her hip. His mouth came down on hers and Angie moaned deep in her throat. Flynn's hand continued its upward journey, pushing the nightgown out of the way until he lifted her to pull it off entirely.

"Angie, honey. I want you so much."

She believed him. The urgency in his husky words came through to her so clearly, appealing to every feminine instinct. The gold seeping into her bloodstream had turned hot under his touch, and she twisted luxuriously, straining against him.

Angie wrapped her arms around Flynn's neck,

opening her mouth to let his tongue invade her intimately. His palm moved over her breast, rasping against the nipples until she cried out softly.

"Do you want me, sweetheart? Tell me you want me."

She told him in a thousand tiny ways. Her nails lightly scored his shoulders and her tongue slipped into his mouth to tease him. She trembled when he caressed her, and when he drew his hand down her stomach to find the dark tangle of hair at the apex of her thighs, she gave him the words in husky, broken little gasps.

"I do want you, Flynn. So much. I've never felt like this, never needed anyone the way I need you tonight."

He drank the words from her lips, clearly taking deep satisfaction from the tremulous confession. She felt the edge of his teeth on her earlobe just as his fingers began to discover her most intimate secrets. Angie shivered with an anticipation that was unlike anything she had ever known.

"You do want me." Flynn's lips were at her throat now. "My God, I can feel how much you need me. You're so warm, so damp and warm. Like hot gold."

How did he know? Angie wondered fleetingly. That was exactly how she felt. The hidden heat in her had surfaced, flowing through every vein, filling her with a reckless wildfire.

"Yes, Flynn. Yes, now, please!"

He groaned hoarsely, needing no further urging. Angie felt herself being pushed deeply into the bedclothes and then Flynn was looming over her, lowering himself heavily along the length of her body. His thighs pushed between hers, and his large hands closed over her shoulders.

She caught her breath as she sensed his hard, blunt manhood waiting at the gate of her softness. And in that timeless second before she gave herself up to his passion, Angie opened her eyes and found his night-darkened gaze burning down into hers.

"Angie, this is right. This is the way it's supposed to be. Trust me, sweetheart."

A part of her was alarmed by the urgency in his words. Then the demands of the moment returned, crashing over both of them in a giant wave. Flynn moved against her, suddenly, completely. Angie gasped as the thrilling shock of his possession rippled through her body. He waited for a few seconds, giving both of them time to absorb the dizzying sensations. Then, with a low, muttered groan, he began to move.

Angie's nails sank more deeply into his shoulders. Her hips lifted in response to the heavy, demanding thrusts of his body. Flynn's name was a soft litany of desire that barely escaped her throat.

The world outside the hotel room ceased to exist for an unmeasured length of time. For Angie there was only the man in whose arms she was so tightly held and the sensual claim he imposed. She could no more deny the flaming need in him than she could have stopped a sweeping brushfire. But her own need was a flame that leaped every bit as high, and the feminine demands she made were answered with a bold eagerness, a fierce, masculine desire to please and satisfy.

And when the end came in a spiral of shimmering excitement that turned on its own axis until it exploded, Angie and Flynn surrendered to it together.

As Angie lay in Flynn's arms, damp and sweetly exhausted and on the verge of sleep, she heard him whisper once more in her ear.

"This is the way it's supposed to be, Angie. I know it. I'm almost home."

Five

Angie awoke to a smoggy Los Angeles sunrise and the certain knowledge that something fundamental had altered in her world during the night. She moved her leg, instinctively seeking Flynn's muscular calf. When she didn't find it she shifted onto her side, trying to find the warmth of his body. During the night she had discovered an enthralling comfort and sense of security in Flynn's arms. It was the sort of thing that could rapidly become addictive, Angie decided. In fact, she had a strong hunch she was already hooked.

Last night had been more than a passionate exploration of the mutual excitement she and Flynn generated in each other. If it had been only that, Angie thought she could have kept it all in some sort of perspective.

It was perfectly true that she had never before

known the kind of passion she'd found during the night, but she was an adult and she thought she could have dealt with physical passion in a mature fashion. At the very least she could have convinced herself not to go off the deep end and tell herself she was in love.

But that sense of comfort and security, that feeling of *belonging* was altogether unexpected and strangely, insidiously alluring.

She tried to tell herself that her emotions were not to be trusted at this stage. The man had probably saved her life. He had most definitely saved the dagger from being stolen. Those facts alone were enough to distort a woman's judgment. Add to them the powerful physical attraction that existed between herself and Flynn, and you had a powder keg of emotions ready to be ignited.

Still, Angie thought she could have handled all those factors in an intelligent, analytical fashion now that morning had arrived. She was, after all, a woman, not a girl. But a sense of perspective remained elusive. And she thought she knew why. The unexpected feeling of rightness that she had experienced in Flynn's arms last night simply refused to be pigeonholed, cataloged or dealt with on a purely intellectual basis. She was falling in love. Perhaps she was already in so deep that fine distinctions didn't matter.

The realization both warmed her and made her uneasy. It left her feeling as though she were standing on a precipice; exposed and vulnerable in a way she had never been before in her life. She stopped seeking Flynn's strong body in the bed and slowly opened her eyes.

"You're awake."

It wasn't, Angie decided, the most loving tone of voice. She turned her head, following the sound of the low, rough words until she saw Flynn. He was fully dressed in the familiar, functional twill pants and a khaki shirt. The scarred leather belt and moccasins seemed as appropriate on him here in L.A. as they had in the exotic atmosphere of the Mexican Caribbean.

He had showered and shaved. Angie had a fleeting memory of the rough texture of his beard as he had cradled her close during the night. Flynn stood by the window, one foot propped on the low ledge shielding the air conditioner that had been installed beneath the glass. He had opened the drapes and had apparently been studying the yellowed horizon until he'd realized she was awake.

"Good morning, Flynn." This opening scene wasn't starting out quite as Angie had expected. During the night she had convinced herself that the morning after would be a time of tenderness and anticipation. But she sensed already that something was going wrong with her imagined scenario. "You're up early. After everything that happened yesterday, I thought you'd want to sleep late this morning." *With me,* she added silently. *I thought you'd want to curl up with me and perhaps make love to me while we teased each other about what to have for breakfast.* Wasn't that what lovers did the morning after?

"Angie, we have to talk."

Real anxiety set in now. Angie sat up slowly, drawing the sheet to her chin in an unconsciously defensive gesture. Her nightgown lay on the floor beside the bed, and she felt more exposed and vulnerable than ever with Flynn standing there fully dressed. She tried to think of something light and brilliant to say and ended up coughing a little to clear her throat first.

"I had no idea you were so chatty first thing in the morning. How about a cup of coffee first?" Did that sound sufficiently careless? Angie's fingers tightened on the hem of the sheet. Oh, God, she wasn't going to be any good at playing careless. She hadn't had the practice.

"We can go downstairs to breakfast later. First we have to get some things clarified between us, Angie." Flynn leaned one elbow casually on his raised knee and looked at her.

With a sickening sense of shock Angie registered the unrelenting grimness of his dark gaze. This was worse than anything she could have imagined. Her pulse began to beat more quickly. She no longer needed a cup of coffee to wake her up, Angie realized. She was suddenly, tensely alert. And her overriding instinct was to run.

Except that of course she couldn't. An image of herself dashing naked out into the hotel corridor brought her back to reality. Drawing a deep, steadying breath, Angie searched for the words that might help her regain a sense of control.

"Don't panic, Flynn. If you're, uh, worrying

about last night...I mean, if you're afraid I'll make a scene or make demands or something..." She was fumbling badly and the knowledge alarmed her. "You don't have to be nervous about my reactions this morning. I know what I said down in Mexico, but I guess I didn't mean it. I'm not going to hurl a lot of accusations or...or blame you for using me. I'm perfectly well aware that what occurred last night was a...a mutual decision and I'm adult enough to—"

"Angie, please shut up." The order was almost gentle, although there was no softness in Flynn's face. "And don't make any promises about not throwing a tantrum until after you've heard what I have to say."

"Flynn, I don't—"

"My name is Flynn Sangrey Challoner, Angie."

She blinked uncertainly as the name worked its way into her brain. "Challoner?"

"That's right. Several generations back one of my ancestors married Maria Isabel Torres. And on the wedding night he discovered his bride had brought a rather unique gift to her new husband."

"The Torres Dagger." Angie couldn't hear any emotion in her own words. They were as dull and flat as she was suddenly feeling.

"Yes." Flynn didn't take his eyes off her face. He looked like a man who has set himself a hard task; a man who won't quit until it's accomplished, regardless of how much pain is involved.

"I see." She couldn't think of anything else to say. Her mind seemed to have gone blank.

"Do you? Angie, I know this is a shock, and I know I've got a lot of explaining to do. But I *can* explain it, honey. That's what I'm trying to do this morning. I want you to understand."

"You want me to understand why you lied to me?"

His dark brows came together in a sudden, fierce frown, and Flynn's jaw hardened. "I haven't lied to you, Angie. I just didn't give you all the facts, because I didn't know how you would react. And I couldn't take a chance on losing track of that dagger again. It's taken me years to trace it this far. When I found I was one step behind someone else who wanted it, I—" He broke off abruptly.

Her chest felt tight, and her nails seemed to be trying to rip through the industrial-strength fabric of the hotel sheet. "Would you mind if I got dressed before we go any further with this?"

The unforgiving angles and planes of Flynn's face seemed to become even harder as he watched her. Angie had the impression he was genuinely torn between granting her reasonable request or making himself look slightly foolish by refusing it. She knew without being told that he wanted to refuse.

"Angie, you're going to listen to me. We're going to get this all out in the open. I know you'll probably be upset at first and I can't blame you, but after I've explained it all you'll understand. Last night you trusted me. And when I've told you all the facts, you'll trust me again."

Her chin lifted as pride twisted through her, cutting across some of the numbness. The pride seemed somehow linked to that temperamental streak of gold that had produced such passion last night. "A gentleman would not mention last night at this stage, Flynn. And a gentleman would go into his room and leave me some privacy in which to get dressed."

"Angie, I want to get this over with as quickly as possible."

"So do I," she whispered fervently. "But I am discovering that it's difficult for a woman to be told she's been a fool while she's sitting naked in bed. Hard on the morale. I'm sure you can understand that. Please leave me alone, Flynn."

He swung his foot down off the air-conditioner ledge and came toward her. "Honey, don't cry. Please don't cry. It's going to be all right. I swear it."

"Don't worry, I have no intention of crying." Her eyes felt hot and bright but she was quite certain she wouldn't cry. That pride was strong stuff. It came to her in a flash of unbidden intuition that Maria Isabel had known such pride.

Flynn hesitated a moment longer, clearly ambivalent about how to handle the situation. He stood at the side of the bed looking down at her and then he nodded abruptly. "Okay. I'll give you a few minutes to get dressed. Are you sure you're all right?"

"Oh, I'm in great shape, Flynn."

He put out a hand to stroke her cheek in a brief caress. Instantly she pulled her face away from his touch. Flynn's hand fell to his side.

"You don't have to be shy with me this morning, Angie. Not after last night."

"Are you going to leave me in peace?"

He exhaled slowly, turned and walked back into his own room. Angie waited until the door closed, and then she fled into the bathroom. She didn't cry in the shower, either. She refused to give in to the impulse, and after a while it faded.

Flynn Sangrey Challoner. The Challoner descendant about whom Uncle Julian had occasionally speculated. Angie stood beneath the steaming water and forced herself to deal with the facts. Everything fit into place so nicely now. The fortunate coincidence of her meeting Flynn in Mexico was completely explained. No wonder Flynn had been so willing to help her at every step along the way.

By the time Angie had finished showering, she only had one real question left to ask Flynn Sangrey Challoner. She coiled her hair into the familiar twist at the nape of her neck, pulled on a pair of pleated black trousers and dug out a slightly wrinkled fuchsia shirt. The strong color contrast gave her a small shot of personal strength. She had a feeling she was going to need it. Already the sense of comfort and security she had discovered during the night had faded into nothingness.

Flynn opened the door between the two rooms just as Angie was closing her suitcase. She glanced at him over her shoulder and then went back to finishing her small task.

"Feel better?" he asked quietly.

"Much. I'm starving, though. Can we have our big conversation over breakfast?" She was proud of the cool way that came out.

"If that's what you want."

"What I'd really like to know is when you intend to steal the dagger."

A shattering silence descended on the room. Angie had a few seconds in which to realize that her single question might have been exceedingly ill-timed. Then Flynn's hand clamped down on her shoulder, and he was spinning her around to face him. She found herself staring up into flint-hard eyes that seemed to burn through her. Several generations of arrogant pride crystalized in that fierce masculine gaze, and for a paralyzing instant Angie felt as if she'd stepped through a time warp and was confronting the reckless, arrogant Challoner who had married Maria Isabel. She went very still beneath the hand that was locked on her shoulder.

"If I had wanted to steal that dagger," Flynn bit out, each word a thrust of the blade, "I could have done it a dozen times since you bought it from Alexander Cardinal. I could have taken it from you and flown out of Mexico with it, and you would have been absolutely helpless to stop me. For that matter I could have taken it last night after you'd fallen asleep so trustingly in my arms. I could have disappeared with it this morning while you were in the shower. I am not a thief, Angie Morgan. My claim on that dagger is more valid than your own or your uncle's, but I will not steal it from you. Before we go a step further, you will apologize to me for your accusation."

Angie found her breath and somehow managed to keep her words under control. She would not surrender to the urge to scream at him. He might have his pride but she had her own, and it was every bit as fierce as his. At any other time that realization would have startled her. But there was no time to consider it now.

"Apologize? To a man who has been deliberately misleading, if not actually lying to me for several days now? Apologize to a man who doesn't even bother to give me his right name before taking me to bed?"

The fingers on her shoulder clenched. "The apology is for the man who saved the dagger and perhaps your life in the process. For the man who didn't steal it although he had plenty of opportunity. The apology, Angie, is for the man you gave yourself to last night. I expect anger from you, and I expect you to feel hurt this morning. You're a woman, and you've got a common ancestry with Maria Isabel. We both know about her temper. I am prepared to put up with a certain amount of temper from you, but I will not allow you to stand there and insult me by calling me a thief. Apologize, damn it!"

Angie didn't need to have it spelled out: she was walking very close to the line. Her accusation had obviously deeply offended Flynn. The logic of the situation was also suddenly inescapable. Flynn hadn't stolen the dagger. Not yet. And she couldn't deny he'd had plenty of opportunity. She drew herself up under his hand.

"My apologies, Mr. Challoner. You have not yet proven yourself a thief. Other things, perhaps, but not a thief."

His eyes narrowed, and she knew he wanted more than that from her. But he must have realized he wouldn't get it. Flynn released her shoulder. "Let's go downstairs and get some coffee."

"And the dagger?" she challenged.

"You can take it with you." He stalked to the door and flung it open, waiting for her.

After a second's pause Angie picked up the dagger's case and followed him out into the hall. All during the long ride down in the elevator she lectured herself on maintaining her control. By the time they reached the lobby cafe Angie felt she had her emotions pushed safely back behind the wall of numbness she had discovered in herself that morning. And she still had her hands on the dagger. It seemed to give her courage.

Not quite enough courage to order a full-course breakfast, she discovered. Her appetite was nonexistent.

"I'll have coffee," she murmured when the waitress came to take their order. It was the first thing Angie had said since leaving the hotel room.

"Angie, you need more than coffee." Flynn glowered at her as he looked up from his menu. "Have some eggs and toast."

"The coffee will be fine."

Flynn turned to the waitress. "We'll both have coffee. We will also each have an order of scrambled eggs and toast."

The waitress didn't wait for confirmation from Angie. She scribbled the order and disappeared in the direction of the kitchen.

Angie shook her head ruefully. "All right, Flynn, you've asserted yourself again, and I don't feel like doing battle over a couple of eggs and toast. I quit, you're the winner. Now will you please say whatever it is you feel obliged to say so we can get this whole thing over with?"

When the waitress returned with their coffee, he picked up his mug and took a deep swallow. Then he set it down with deliberation. "Angie, everything I told you in Mexico was the truth. The only thing I left out was my last name."

"Looking back, I'd say that was a rather major omission."

He sighed. "I know," he surprised her by saying bleakly. "But I didn't have much choice. Not in the beginning. Angie, I've been trying to trace that dagger for nearly eight years. I've spent a great deal of money having antique weapons specialists search gallery catalogs and private collections looking for the Torres Dagger. I didn't know your uncle was out there looking for it, too. In fact, I didn't even know your uncle existed until I finally got word that someone else had also been trying to track the dagger. By then it was too late. Julian Torres had already had more luck than I'd had. He'd located Alexander Cardinal and made an offer. Word was he'd offered a lot more than I could afford, even if I could have convinced Cardinal to deal with me instead. I learned through an antique dealer who had helped your uncle locate the dagger that Torres was going down to Mexico to collect it."

"And you decided to follow," Angie concluded evenly.

"Yes. I'm not sure exactly what I hoped to accomplish, but I had to see the dagger for myself, so I followed and found you instead of Julian Torres. It wasn't hard making certain I'd found the right person. You talked willingly enough about why you were in Mexico."

Angie smiled without any trace of humor. "So I did. You talked a lot about why you were there, too, as I recall. You said you were on vacation."

Flynn shrugged. "I was in a sense."

"Resting between engagements," she said, reminding him of the phrase he had used.

He gave her a steady look. "It was the truth."

She picked up her coffee with an uneasy feeling. "I don't think I ever asked you exactly what kind of engagements you meant."

"No, you were afraid to ask, weren't you?"

"Perhaps I just didn't want to embarrass you," she suggested calmly.

"I don't think that was it. I think you were protecting yourself. You didn't want to know for certain if your suspicions about the way I made my living were correct. But you must have been fairly sure of your guess or you wouldn't have asked me to escort you to Cardinal's island that night."

Angie took another sip of coffee. He was right in some ways. She hadn't really wanted to hear it put into words. "I think I can handle it now. Why don't you try telling me the truth?"

He looked briefly down at his hands, which were

wrapped around his coffee mug. Then he raised his eyes to meet hers. "Your guesses were all probably quite accurate."

She winced but said nothing.

"Angie, I've lived a little rough these past few years. But I'm alive, I've made some money and I haven't done anything of which I'm ashamed. There's no need to go into it in any further detail."

"I agree."

His mouth hardened. "Since you were willing to commission my services as a bodyguard that night when you went to Cardinal's island, it's a bit hypocritical of you to act as if you find my past dishonorable or disgusting."

She met his eyes. "I didn't avoid the subject of your past because I found it dishonorable or disgusting. I might not like the idea of how you make your living, but I wouldn't use words such as *dishonorable* or *disgusting* to describe it. And you're quite right. It would be hypocritical of me since I did plan to use your, uh, skills that night. In fact, your skills came in very handy when Cousin Ramon pulled that Star semiautomatic."

Curiosity flickered briefly in his eyes at her identification of the weapon, but he ignored that question to ask the more important one. "If you don't find my background repellent, why did you work so hard at avoiding the subject?"

Angie toyed with her spoon, unnecessarily stirring her coffee. "Because thinking about the way you made your living only reinforced the impossibility of our having any kind of future. I assumed that men who lived a little rough, as you put it, probably don't have much room in their lives for anything other than vacation flings.''

Flynn's hand came across the short space that separated them. It closed over her restlessly moving fingers, stilling the spoon in the cup. ''That assumption doesn't hold true for me, Angie. I've got plans for the future, and they don't include going back to selling myself as a bodyguard or offering my services to people who find their relatives locked up in strange jails in countries that have never heard of due process of law.''

She bit her lip. ''Is that the sort of thing you did?''

He ignored the question, leaning forward intently. ''Angie, I've got a past, but not the one you're thinking of. My past goes back to a time when the Challoners owned land and bred strong sons to inherit that land. It goes back to a time when a family knew its roots and knew the source of its strength. A time when a man and a woman respected that kind of strength and were willing to work hard to make it even stronger.''

She felt the intensity in him and experienced a kind of wonder. ''All those things you said in Mexico about the importance of families and their ties to the land, you really believe all that, don't you?''

''I believe it. I'm going to rebuild what the Challoners once had, Angie. I'm going to make the family strong again.''

''I've got news for you, Flynn, the cattle business isn't what it used to be. If you're thinking of starting a ranch in California, you're in for a surprise. You'd probably be better off raising chickens than cattle. No glamour, I suppose, but the fact is, people eat more chicken these days. Better yet, try oil wells. Now, there's a surefire crop.''

Flynn released her hand and sat back in his chair as the plates of eggs and toast were delivered to the table. His dark eyes were gleaming with that unyielding determination she had seen earlier. It was unnerving, Angie thought. She poked idly at the scrambled eggs, thinking of the other things Flynn had said when he had discussed family history. The notion of a business marriage had seemed perfectly rational to him, she recalled. Anything that helped strengthen the family holdings. It struck her that Flynn Challoner was living in the wrong century.

Across the table Flynn picked up his fork and attacked his scrambled eggs. ''I'm not going to raise cattle the way my ancestors did. And you can forget chicken farming. But the key is still the land, Angie. I'm sure of it. I feel it deep inside. But this is a new era and I understand that the land has to be handled in different ways.''

Angie couldn't resist asking, ''What ways?''

''You buy it and you sell it,'' he said with great simplicity.

She eyed him uncertainly. ''I don't get it. Speculation?''

He shook his head. ''It's not speculation when you know what you're doing. It's a certainty. That's the thing about land, honey. It's forever. It'll take care of the man who takes care of it. The man who knows what he's doing.''

"Have you done much, uh, buying and selling?"

"I've been putting every spare cent I've had during the past few years into my first holdings. I just kept sending the money to a bank account in the States, and whenever I had enough I'd fly back and figure out where to put it. I've got a little property in the Sun Belt and some on the water in Oregon and Washington. It's not much, but it's a start. I've already sold one or two parcels in some growth areas in the Pacific Northwest and down in Arizona. Made a good return on my investment and sank the results right back into more land. I've got a long way to go and God knows right now I'm cash poor, but I've got the basis for a beginning. I can live on what the land makes now. And that's enough. I'm back in the States for good this time. Now I can really start to build."

Angie felt her stomach tighten. She put down her fork. "And the dagger?"

He paused, a bite of egg halfway to his mouth. "The dagger is part of the whole process, Angie. It's part of the past and the present and the future. Don't you see? It helps tie it all together. It's a link. A symbol."

"And you want it."

"I want it," he agreed flatly.

Angie massaged her temple with her thumb. "How on earth did I get mixed up in this?" she whispered more to herself than to him.

"You're mixed up in it because you're part of the whole thing, too, honey. I didn't realize it when I followed you to Mexico but now I do. And that's what I wanted to tell you this morning. I know that I probably should have told you last night before—''

"Before you seduced me? Yes, it might have been the polite thing to do."

"Angie, I was afraid you wouldn't understand or that you'd be so furious you wouldn't give me a chance to fully explain. I don't expect you to believe this, but after making love to you I stayed awake most of the night wondering if I'd done the right thing." Flynn's gaze didn't waver.

"Really? And what did you decide?"

"I decided that it was probably safer to have played my hand the way I did, even if it did leave me feeling guilty." His voice was suddenly harsh.

She stared at him. "Played your hand?"

"I wanted to make the bonds between us as strong as possible before I took the risk of telling you everything. Don't you see? I knew how you felt about the dagger and about your past. You'd made it very clear that none of it had much meaning to you. I couldn't risk appealing to you on that basis. But I also knew that you were attracted to me, and I had a hunch you were the kind of woman who would commit herself to a man when she let him make love to her. You were already grateful to me for helping you get the dagger safely out of Mexico. I figured that if I could reinforce that by making you feel committed on a more intimate level..." His voice trailed off meaningfully.

Angie felt the color surge into her cheeks. "You don't need to continue. I get the point. You thought you could control me emotionally through sex."

His fork clattered on his plate, drawing a curious

glance from the next table. "Damn it," Flynn snapped, "that's not it at all."

"You'll have to excuse me, I'm having a little difficulty understanding all the fine nuances of the thing."

His eyes softened for the first time that morning. "Angie, honey, do you remember what I told you last night when I came to your bed?"

She refused to answer on the grounds that she might have lost her self-control.

Flynn smiled gently. "I told you everything was going to be all right. That this was the way it was supposed to be. I'm sure of it, Angie. I trust my own instincts in this."

"That's very reassuring, naturally..."

"Don't be flippant, honey. You don't have to be defensive. I want you to know that everything *is* all right. That nothing has changed."

"Except that now you're going to take the dagger and stroll off into the sunset?"

"At this point your uncle owns that dagger."

"I'm glad we agree on something, at least."

Flynn brushed aside her brittle response, the cool determination returning to his eyes. "I intend to drive up the coast with you and meet Julian Torres. He and I will talk about the dagger and what happens next. From what you've told me, I think your uncle understands what that dagger means. And since he and I seem to be the sole surviving males on each side of the family, it's up to us to settle the matter."

"What if he doesn't want to talk to you?" But Angie was grasping at straws and she knew it. Julian would be utterly fascinated to meet the surviving member of the Challoner clan; doubly fascinated when he learned that Flynn Sangrey Challoner had spent a good portion of his life living the kind of adventures Jake Savage undertook within the pages of the Julian Taylor novels. Above all else, her uncle loved tales that came to life.

"Judging by what you've told me of your uncle, he'll want to talk to me." Flynn sounded very certain. "As Cardinal said, he sounds like a man who understands the importance of family ties and family history."

She was the only one who seemed to be left out in the cold, standing by while the men decided the fate of the dagger. This was probably very much how Maria Isabel had felt when she'd heard that her own fate was being decided nearly two hundred years ago. In fact, something deep inside Angie was quite certain this was how Maria Isabel had felt.

Luckily this was the twentieth century, Angie thought. The men could haggle over an antique, but they couldn't very well make decisions concerning the future of a woman.

She silently repeated the bit of wisdom several times during breakfast, but for some reason Angie didn't manage to reassure herself. Flynn had said he wanted to recreate the Challoner dynasty. The land and the dagger were a start.

The next thing on his shopping list was going to be a woman.

Six

Flynn realized that what he was feeling was an overwhelming sense of relief. She'd handled it well, he told himself as he piloted the red Toyota out of the Los Angeles area and started north along the coast. Initially she'd been a little shaken, there was no doubt about that, but it could have been a lot worse.

He'd expected tears, a tantrum, a lot of yelling and screaming. After all, as he'd learned during the night, Angie was a woman of passion. She was a Torres woman, he thought, not without a sense of pride.

But she'd been surprisingly calm when he'd finally told her the whole truth about himself. And for that, Flynn Sangrey Challoner was very, very grateful.

He hadn't lied when he'd told her that he lay

awake a good portion of the night trying to decide how to reveal who he really was. He hadn't meant to let the misconception go so far. But there had been no really appropriate time to explain.

Down in Mexico he had wanted to secure her trust and friendship. If he'd announced his identity to her, she would have been immediately wary of him. He'd had no way of knowing how she would react if she suspected he might be planning to cut his own deal with Alexander Cardinal. It was a cinch she would never have let him get close to her.

He'd planned to tell her yesterday during the trip home, but there had been so much going on and they had both been so exhausted. Besides, Angie had been badly shaken by the scene with Ramon. It hadn't seemed an auspicious time for true confessions. Then last night he'd realized why he'd been putting off the hour of reckoning. On first a subconscious and then a very conscious level Flynn knew he'd wanted to strengthen the bonds between himself and Angie before telling her exactly who he was.

He'd tormented himself for hours after they'd checked into the airport hotel. Alone in his own room he'd sat in the chair by the window, the lights out, gazing at the city's night skyline. A myriad disconnected thoughts had gone through his head. He was close to the dagger at last. After working so hard and so long to trace it, victory had remained elusive, however.

It wasn't simply that the weapon technically belonged to Julian Torres. It was far more complicated than that. Somehow, Flynn wasn't quite certain why, the dagger was now inevitably connected in his mind with Angie Morgan. It had struck him there in the darkness that he no longer wanted only the cold steel with its gem-encrusted handle. He wanted the woman whose touch could warm the steel.

Angie and the dagger went together, and when he had them both he would have the real foundation for everything he planned to build in the future.

Sitting there in the darkness, Flynn could not explain to himself precisely why he was so certain that he needed both the woman and the dagger to make it all complete. Perhaps it had something to do with the fact that Angie was of the Torres clan and the dagger had originally come to the Challoners through a Torres woman. The explanation fit, he decided. It all went together to make a perfect circle. The symmetry of the whole thing pleased him on some fundamental level. Angie, the dagger and a new beginning.

It was then that he knew he would have to tell her the truth about himself in the morning. He wanted everything out in the open. The deception he'd been practicing for the past few days, however much he could justify it, disturbed him. He didn't like the feeling of guilt that was eating at him. He was an honorable man, and he wanted his association with Angie put on an honorable basis. His Challoner pride demanded it.

But she was a woman and she was part Torres. He was afraid she would not easily forgive him. After all, if the situation had been reversed, how would he behave? The thought didn't bear contemplation. Flynn knew what his own reactions would have been if he'd perceived himself the victim of this kind of deception. He would have been madder than hell.

So, he told himself determinedly, he had to expect fury; a woman's fury. Before he could risk that he had to strengthen the bonds of attraction that shimmered between them. Sitting there at two o'clock in the morning it had all seemed so entirely logical.

When he'd finally walked into her room he'd had a few more doubts, but when she'd opened her arms to him any last-minute hesitation he might have had was gone in the blaze of passion that had consumed him. This was right; the way it was supposed to be. He knew it deep inside.

As he sat behind the wheel of the Toyota, Flynn's body still reacted to the memory of Angie in the night. He felt himself tighten and had to consciously force himself to relax. She had melted in his hands last night. He had been dazed by the hot, sweet excitement, unexpectedly and totally out of control. And he had fit her the way the dagger fit its sheath.

Afterward the reality of what had to be done in the morning had returned. As if to ward off the inevitable, Flynn had pulled the sleeping Angie closer against him. And all through the sleepless night she had lain trusting in his arms.

But now as they left the smog-laden air of Los Angeles behind, Flynn allowed himself to breathe a sigh of relief. It was going to be all right. Angie had accepted the situation. He'd been right to handle it the way he had. Last night had meant something very special to her, too, and because of it she was dealing with this morning's news with more equanimity than he had expected.

Relief made him feel conversational. She hadn't talked to him a lot since they had left the hotel. She didn't seem hostile, though, just quiet. He slanted her a glance, studying her profile as she sat gazing meditatively out the window.

The fall sun was brilliant on the ocean but the warmth in the air felt temporary. It would disappear quickly after sunset when the coastal fog moved inward. With the sprawl of Los Angeles well behind them, the real California seemed to emerge. Parts of the drive cut through land that still looked very much as it had when the Torres and Challoner families began building their ranching empires. Rolling hills still met the Pacific in timeless intimacy. That was the thing about land, Flynn thought with deep satisfaction. You could plant it, ranch it, subdivide it or build cities on it. But regardless of what you did to it, it continued to exist. It would continue to take care of the man who valued it.

He wondered what Angie was thinking as she sat pensively in her seat. Her beautiful peacock eyes were shadowed with private thoughts. Not for the first time he recalled her bravery in Ramon's boat. He respected that kid of courage and quick thinking. But when he thought about Angie's actions he experienced more than respect: he knew a deep sense of pride in her. He was honest enough with himself to realize it was because he was already thinking of her as his. *His woman had courage.*

"There's something I've been meaning to ask you," Flynn said at one point. She flashed him a quick glance but said nothing. "This morning you mentioned the gun Ramon used. How did you know it was a Star?"

She hesitated. "You once told me you admired the technical side of the Jake Savage books."

He nodded, curious.

"Well," she continued, "who do you think usually gets stuck doing the technical research?"

"You?" He was startled. The Jake Savage series was high adventure with plenty of detail concerning the various lethal gadgets used by the hero.

"Me." She didn't pursue the subject. "The road to Julian's place is just a few miles outside of Ventura. We'll be there shortly."

"How far is the hacienda from your uncle's home?"

"A couple of miles. It sits on a bluff overlooking the sea. The guest house is a few hundred yards away from it."

Angie saw the interest in Flynn's eyes as he scanned the landscape. Was he imagining how this country had looked back when the Challoners and the Torreses had reigned? In many ways he seemed hard and cynical; a man who had seen nearly everything. Yet when he talked of the land and his plans for the future, there was a genuine kind of anticipation and determination in him; a sense of respect and hope for the future. She had been aware of it at breakfast when he'd explained his goals, and she could feel it emanating from him now as he drove toward his meeting with Julian Torres.

It disturbed her that she was sensitive to his feelings about the land and the future. She didn't want to be, Angie realized. She wanted to keep her distance from him emotionally. She didn't want to be seen by Flynn as a part of his plans.

Her uncle had been first astounded and then delighted when she'd phoned earlier to say that she was on her way with a genuine Challoner in tow. He'd assured her he had fully recovered from his bout with the flu and that he would be expecting them that afternoon. He would instruct Mrs. Akers, the housekeeper, to plan dinner for three.

"This is wonderful, Angie," Julian had said enthusiastically. "Absolutely wonderful. What an incredible coincidence that you should run into Challoner down in Mexico."

Looking at Flynn, who was pacing the hotel room while she made the call, Angie had murmured dryly into the phone, "Uncle Julian, you know what Jake Savage always says about coincidences."

Julian Torres had chuckled richly. "I should know, I've written it often enough." He pitched his voice low and gravelly as he muttered, "There ain't no such thing."

"Exactly. Keep it in mind. We'll see you this afternoon, Uncle Julian."

And now they were almost there. In quiet tones Angie gave directions to Flynn, who turned off the main highway to follow a narrow road that wound through a small residential area composed of secluded, expensive homes. A grove of trees protected the modern glass-and-wood structure Julian was calling home until the hacienda was finished. The house had a spectacular view of the sea. Down below it a ragged cliff descended to a quiet beach. The other homes in the area were equally secluded. Privacy was a valued commodity along this expensive strip of land, and people who could afford it were willing to pay well for the luxury. The author of the wonderfully successful Jake Savage books could afford it.

Flynn parked the Toyota in the paved drive, glancing around at the lush garden.

"Julian designed the garden a couple of years ago," Angie said politely. "He's a whiz with plants and flowers."

Flynn nodded just as the wrought-iron gates swung open and a pleasantly distinguished, middle-aged man came through to greet them. Julian still had a full head of hair, and in true California style, he kept himself trim with exercise and a healthy diet, supplemented by the medicinal properties of good Spanish sherry. He was dressed casually but expensively, and there was an air of West Coast sophistication about him.

"Angelina," Julian Torres said grandly, "you're finally here. How was the trip?" He was the only one who ever called her by her full name.

"Eventful." She hugged her uncle. "You're looking great considering you've just gotten over the flu."

"It turned out to be a fairly mild case. I dosed myself with plenty of sherry and hardly felt a thing." He looked appraisingly at Flynn. "Introduce us, Angelina."

"Julian, I'd like you to meet Flynn Sangrey...Challoner." She paused just a split second before drawing out Flynn's last name, and she saw him glance at her coolly as he shook hands with the other man.

"We've been a long while reuniting the Challoners and the Torreses, Flynn. It's about time," Julian said with satisfaction as he assessed the younger man. "Come inside. We have a lot to talk about. You can't imagine how pleased I am to meet you."

"I think I'll just play solitaire or something this evening," Angie murmured. "I don't think you're going to need me in this discussion."

Flynn came up behind her before Julian could answer. Angie felt his strong hand at the base of her spine, guiding her into the house in a proprietary fashion. "Whatever we talk about tonight will definitely involve you, Angie. You're part of the past."

She had wanted to argue that point, but there was no real opportunity. With typical graciousness Julian served dark, rich coffee and small, spicy empanadas Mrs. Akers sent out from the kitchen. Angie would have felt rude and ridiculously uncivilized if she'd made a scene at that point. Then, his dark eyes alive with anticipation, Julian asked to see the dagger.

"It's in my suitcase," Angie said. She rose to her feet. "I'll get it." With a sense of relief at being able to escape the mutual admiration society that seemed to be developing between her uncle and Flynn, she hurried out to the car. There she unlocked the Toyota's trunk and opened the suitcase. Reaching inside she picked up the dagger's case. For a moment, standing there alone, she held it in her hands and wondered again at the sense of possessiveness she felt.

This weapon had belonged to Maria Isabel. It had been handed over to the Challoners a very long time ago, but now it was back in the hands of a Torres woman. True, Angie thought, her connection with Maria Isabel was vague and quite distant, but still, she was the one who now held the dagger Maria Isabel had once possessed.

Uneasily Angie shook off the strange sensation that gripped her each time she touched the dagger. She was letting her imagination get the better of her. Determinedly she stalked back into the house carrying the case. Walking up to Julian, she opened it and displayed the object of the quest on which he had sent her.

Silently Flynn came up beside Julian and watched as the dagger was revealed. There was a moment of silence during which Julian's face reflected the unmitigated satisfaction he was feeling.

"It's beautiful," he said at last. "And it looks exactly as it was described in the family papers." Carefully he lifted it out of the box and removed it from the old leather sheath. "Go fetch Mrs. Akers. She'll want to see it, too. It cost me a fortune, but it was worth every cent."

Angie slipped into the kitchen and made a face at

the bustling, silver-haired woman who took care of her uncle's home. "Your presence has been requested, Mrs. Akers. You are to appear in the living room and make appropriately appreciative sounds."

"About that dagger?" The pleasant-faced woman chuckled, dusting the pastry flour off her hands. "Don't worry, I'll make a proper scene. Your uncle has talked of little else since you left last week. And when he heard you were returning with a genuine Challoner, well, I haven't seen him looking so satisfied since his agent negotiated that last contract with his publisher." She obediently followed Angie out into the living room, expressed the required admiration for the dagger and then excused herself on the grounds that a pie required her attention.

Julian frowned at Flynn. "Cardinal didn't give you any trouble?"

Flynn shrugged. "Not when we made the transaction, but there was a little trouble later on. It's a long story."

"From the correspondence I've had with him, I assumed the man was a gentleman," Julian said abruptly. "I never would have allowed Angie to go down there alone otherwise."

"I made the same assumption," Flynn admitted. "But someone tried to get the dagger back before we got out of Mexico. I'm afraid we left in something of a rush. Angie's sure Cardinal was behind what happened."

"Let's have the whole story," Julian insisted. With a serious expression on his face he set down the dagger case and picked up his coffee cup.

"It was very exciting, Uncle Julian. You would have loved it." Angie crossed her ankles and leaned back in her chair. Resting her elbows on the upholstered arms, she steepled her fingers and smiled aloofly. "Plenty of material in it for a Julian Taylor novel. Even had our own Jake Savage on the scene to handle the bad guy."

Flynn shifted restlessly in his chair by the window. "Maybe I'd better tell this story. Angie seems inclined to embellish." In a matter-of-fact way he related the incidents leading up to their hasty departure from Mexico. Before he had finished Julian was looking shocked.

"Thank God you were there with her, Flynn. It could have been disastrous if Angelina had been forced to deal with that Ramon character on her own." Julian turned to Angie. "You're quite all right?"

"Oh, I'm fine. The real excitement came later."

Across the room Flynn narrowed his gaze warningly.

Angie went on as if she hadn't gotten the hint. "I was quite surprised to find out who Flynn really was. You see, up until that point I was under the impression his name was Flynn Sangrey."

There was a moment of silence in the room, and then Julian looked questioningly at Flynn. Flynn drummed his fingers briefly on the arm of his chair and, in turn, looked at Angie.

"I didn't know who she was at first," he said quietly. "And when I found out, I wasn't at all sure how she'd react to my presence down there in Mexico. I thought she would be suspicious. Wary of me. Afraid I was after the dagger.''

''Aren't you?'' Angie asked. She smiled her aloof, fleeting smile.

It was Julian who answered very calmly, ''Of course he is. His family has as much claim on it, if not more, than ours.''

''Not any longer,'' Angie said. ''You own it now, Julian. You've bought and paid for it.''

Julian's mouth crooked slightly. ''But Flynn rescued it when it was threatened by your friend Ramon and whoever he was working for. That more than restores his claim, I should think. And I believe I understand completely why he was hesitant to tell you exactly who he was. He would have risked losing track of the dagger again if you had run off in panic without him. Isn't that right, Flynn?''

''Something like that.'' Laconically, Flynn smiled at Angie. ''But in the end she took the news very calmly. I was probably wrong to be so concerned.''

Julian shook his head. ''No. Not when you'd spent such a long time searching for it, Flynn. You're not wrong to tread carefully when you finally close in on the object of the hunt.''

Angie watched them, withdrawing into silence as the two men began to talk freely about the dagger and its history. There were questions about Flynn's history, too, and she noticed he only provided brief answers. His responses were enough to intrigue Julian, however. Angie knew her uncle was starting to see him just as she had suspected he would see Flynn: as a real-life version of Jake Savage.

It was obvious, though, that his former method of making a living wasn't what Flynn wanted to talk about. It was when the discussion got around to his future plans that he sat forward in his chair and became very intent.

"As I was telling Angie this morning, I've got a start in land. I think the next step is to set up a sort of syndicate of investors. It takes big money to buy the best land. I've been feeling my way for a few years, and I think I'm ready to go ahead with some major investment plans. I intend to pool the cash from a few investors and make the decisions about which parcels to pick up and when to sell them off. Land is still the key to everything, Julian. Just as it was two hundred years ago. Today even the new hotshot computer firms need land and buildings. It doesn't matter how high tech a company is, it can't get very far if it isn't sitting on prime real estate. Agriculture still takes vast amounts of land. That will never change. Residential housing, shopping centers, high-rise office buildings, everything requires land. It always comes back to the land. And I think I've got a feel for it."

Time passed as the men talked. Eventually the sun lavishly painted the western sky as it disappeared into the Pacific, and Julian genially announced that the cocktail hour had finally arrived. He poured sherry and Mrs. Akers sent out quesadillas. Angie nibbled on the cheese-filled tortillas and sipped at her drink, waiting for dinner. No one seemed concerned that she had slipped out of the conversation.

She wondered when someone would ask Flynn where he intended to stay for the night.

When the subject finally arose it didn't come in the form of a question. Julian had apparently already considered the matter and come to a decision. It was announced over dinner.

"I don't know whether Angie mentioned it or not, Flynn, but the hacienda is close to completion. There's furniture in the master bedroom and the kitchen and living room areas. Also the electricity is on and the plumbing works. There's no reason someone couldn't spend a few nights there if he didn't mind stepping over some odds and ends left behind by the designer and the craftspeople. What do you say? Would you like to stay there instead of bunking down here or finding a motel?"

"That's very generous of you," Flynn observed, not looking at Angie.

Julian looked up from his shellfish pilaf. "You'd be doing me a favor, you know. I've been uneasy about Angelina moving into the guest house all by herself. That stretch of beach is a bit isolated. It would be good to know you were nearby. I won't be ready to move in until next month. Didn't want to disrupt the book I'm working on at the moment."

Angie glanced up sharply, but she wasn't in time to halt Flynn's quietly enthusiastic response.

"I'd like that," he said. "I'd like to see what you've done with the old place. The site of the original Torres hacienda, hmm?"

"Took us a while to authenticate it," Julian told him, "but we're sure of it now. The old land records were still available. From what we can tell, the spot where the Challoner place stood was a few miles inland.''

Flynn nodded. ''There's nothing left of it now. I drove out there once to look for some signs of a foundation or something but I couldn't find anything. Belongs to some horse breeder. Can't complain, I guess. At least he didn't put in a subdivision. I don't mind good Arabians running over it.''

''True,'' Julian agreed philosophically. ''You know it was at the hacienda that your ancestor met Maria Isabel the first time. It was at a huge fiesta her father was giving for everyone in the territory. He even invited his enemies, the Challoners, who graciously stopped quarreling with him long enough to stuff themselves on Torres beef.''

Flynn laughed. ''Never let it be said that a Challoner doesn't know when to take advantage of a good thing.''

Angie spoke up for the first time in half an hour. ''I believe that's exactly what Maria Isabel is reputed to have told Curtis Challoner the night of the fiesta. Isn't that how the story goes, Uncle Julian?''

''Something like that,'' Julian agreed cheerfully as he poured more wine in everyone's glass. ''She apparently put it into more forceful terms, though. Walked up to Challoner while he was finishing a bottle of her father's fabulously expensive wine, which had been brought all the way from Spain, and proceeded to insult the man. Told him he was obviously nothing more than a freeloading peasant with aspirations above his station. Or words to that effect. Probably sounded much better in Spanish. Or much worse, depending on your point of view. At any rate the insult was considered outrageous since it had taken place during a time of truce when Challoner was a guest in the Torres home. Maria Isabel was reported to be a little spitfire. A real handful.''

"Spoiled rotten, no doubt," Flynn decided as he helped himself to another serving of asparagus.

Angie felt obliged to speak up again. "She was a woman living in a man's world, and there were no doubt times she resented the situation. I don't blame her at all. Curtis Challoner, from all reports, was arrogant, ambitious and quite ruthless.''

"Well, whatever the rights and wrongs of the situation," Julian interrupted, "that was the occasion on which Challoner informed Torres that he would be willing to take his daughter off his hands if it would resolve the land issue.''

"How generous of him," Angie grumbled.

A savagely amused grin crossed Flynn's face briefly. "According to my family's side of the story, what he actually said to Maria Isabel was that the freeloading peasant was going to do her a favor. He promised to turn her from a willful little tigress into a loving wife and mother. She responded by telling him she would see him in hell first. He told her he'd heard wedding nights described in many ways but not as hell. However, he had confidence she had an original turn of mind and he looked forward to the occasion just to see what she would come up with.''

"And what she came up with was the Torres Dagger," Angie finished triumphantly.

"Cold steel and a warm woman make an interesting combination." Flynn smiled blandly and held out the bread basket. "Have some more jalapeno corn bread."

Aware that Julian was watching her with ill-concealed curiosity, Angie politely accepted the hot-pepper-flavored corn bread and sank back into silence.

"How long will you be staying in the area?" Julian inquired, looking at Flynn.

"Until I can talk you out of that dagger." Flynn took a long swallow of the wine and regarded the last male Torres. "What'll it take?"

Julian leaned back and arched one brow. A strange smile lurked deep in his eyes. "To talk me out of the dagger? I'm not sure. I'll have to think about it. I've worked very long and very hard to get it, Flynn."

"So have I."

Julian nodded complacently. "And your claim on it is as strong as my own. I realize that. It's not going to be a simple decision."

"I can't better the price you paid Alexander Cardinal for it," Flynn said with blunt honesty. "Not right now. I've got some property that I could sell to raise that kind of cash, but to tell you the truth, that land shouldn't be sold. Not yet."

"The dagger isn't something that should be bought and sold between a Torres and a Challoner anyway, is it, Flynn?"

"No," Flynn agreed. "It's not. It means too much."

Angie absorbed the implications of those words. She saw the look that was exchanged between her uncle and Flynn and she knew that with some silent, male form of communication they were arriving at a conclusion. Firmly she squashed the wave of uncertainty that assailed her. She was not Maria Isabel. She didn't have to panic. *But Maria Isabel had not only panicked, she'd been enraged.* Angie suddenly knew that as surely as if she'd been told by Maria Isabel, herself. A little shakily she put down her fork and reached for her wineglass.

Nothing more was said about the dagger at dinner that night, but by the end of the meal Angie was convinced that forces already in motion were moving toward some inevitable conclusion that involved her. She was aware of a vague sense of being trapped, and she wondered if this was how Maria Isabel had felt.

Irritably she pushed aside the bizarre question. This was ridiculous. She was a woman of the twentieth century, and she would not allow herself to be used by two men who were looking for a way to resolve ownership of an inanimate object.

Besides, she reminded herself grimly, nobody had exactly asked her to martyr herself in marriage, anyway. Talk about jumping the gun! The thought brought a reluctant smile to her lips.

"Something funny?" Flynn asked.

"A private joke."

"Going to share it?" he prodded.

"I've already shared it."

He eyed her narrowly. "With whom?"

"Maria Isabel."

Seven

He hadn't planned on waking up alone.

Three days after his return to California with Angie, Flynn opened his eyes in the master bedroom of the hacienda and glared evilly at the bright morning light streaming through the window. He came alert as he always did, fully and completely, with no lazy middle ground between sleep and wakefulness. Wondering if that habit would change now that he was back in the States for good, Flynn shoved aside the quilt and sat up on the edge of the huge carved-wood bed.

Julian Torres had spared no expense in rebuilding the hacienda. Nor had he made the mistake of going overboard on authenticity. The place was ·intended to be a home, not a museum. Windows were larger and more plentiful than they had been in the original hacienda because twentieth-century Californians prized their views. There was air-conditioning and central heating, although the architectural focus in the living room and master suite was on the magnificent fireplaces. A beautifully landscaped courtyard was another main focus. The furniture was comfortable and in most cases new, although it had been carefully chosen to recreate the original Spanish ambience. Heavy-beamed ceilings were combined with walls that had been finished to resemble white-painted adobe. Hardwood floors and some very expensive tile work extended throughout the home.

The whole effect, although modern in many ways, called to mind the elegantly warm, uncluttered effect of the Spanish colonial style. Flynn had felt comfortably at home right from the start. He had said so to Angie that first night when he'd driven her back from Julian's.

"But it's not your home. It's a Torres home," she'd reminded him coolly as she'd shown him through the house.

"The Torres and Challoner families were linked together after the marriage between Curtis and Maria Isabel. After that the homes of each were always open to the other." He'd tried to gently emphasize that point but she hadn't seemed to be listening. Flynn had reached out to catch her wrist as she attempted to walk past him into the kitchen. Smiling slightly and pleasantly aware of the uncoiling anticipation in his body, he'd tugged her into his arms. *"Mi casa es su casa.* It's been a long day, honey. You must be exhausted."

"Not nearly as long as yesterday." She'd slipped out of his hands and walked on into the kitchen. "Mrs. Akers told Uncle Julian she didn't want a two-hundred-year-old kitchen. She insisted on all the latest appliances. But the architect did a good job of hiding everything, don't you think? And look at the tile work along the counter. That was done by a wonderful artist from Santa Barbara."

"Angie…"

"Wait until you see the view in the morning. Absolutely fabulous. There's a path down the cliff to the beach if you want to go for an early morning walk. I usually do."

"Angie, I'll build a fire in the fireplace…"

"Uncle Julian hasn't gotten around to ordering the wood yet."

"Well, maybe a glass of sherry or something."

"There aren't any supplies in the kitchen yet, either." She'd smiled politely, a hint of triumph in her eyes as she succeeded in stonewalling him. She waited for the next suggestion.

It had taken a few more attempts before Flynn realized Angie had no intention of staying with him that night. She was still a little upset over the morning's revelations, he'd decided. She needed time to accept the situation. At least she wasn't actively fighting him. She just needed time, and he was willing to be patient. After all, he'd already waited for years to gather the foundations of the next Challoner dynasty. He could wait a little longer.

When he'd eventually reconciled himself to the fact that she didn't intend to spend the night, Flynn had walked Angie to the guest cottage. It was then that he had understood Julian's concerns.

"This place really is isolated, Angie." He'd surveyed the cottage's location, noting that, while one could see the lights of the main house some distance away, there was no other place within shouting distance. The next home on the cliff was out of sight. "You shouldn't have moved in here until your uncle was ready to move into the hacienda."

"I didn't want to wait. Besides, my lease was up on the place I was renting in Ventura. The cottage was finished first, several weeks before the hacienda, so I decided to move in."

"You could have stayed at your uncle's house until the hacienda was ready." Disapprovingly Flynn had examined the small, one-bedroom arrangement from the living room door. Angie hadn't invited him any further into the cottage.

"Why would I want to live with my uncle? I'm a big girl now. I told you, I like my privacy."

That had really annoyed him. "It's not safe."

"Flynn, I'm twenty-eight years old. I've been living on my own a long time. This isn't the 1800s when single women were expected to live under the family roof until they married."

There had been a hint of a challenge in her peacock eyes, and Flynn had almost made the mistake of accepting it. Then he'd realized she was primed for a clash of wills. Telling himself that the last thing he wanted to do was provide her with an excuse for an argument, he'd backed down. The bond between them was still fragile, and he hadn't wanted to do anything to destabilize the situation.

Now, three days later, Flynn was broodingly aware that he couldn't figure out what in hell was going through Angie's head. If he pushed her too hard, the flare of defiance leaped into her eyes. But if he kept his distance emotionally, she seemed content to have him around.

It was unsettling and confusing, and it was becoming downright maddening. He didn't even know for certain if she was deliberately playing some kind of game. It had crossed his mind that she might want to punish him for the deception he had practiced in Mexico, but he'd decided he was mistaken when no screaming tirade had materialized. But if she wasn't plotting revenge, what was she doing?

Things had been much simpler in the old days, Flynn decided morosely as he got up from the bed and padded over to the window. Curtis Challoner hadn't had to deal directly with Maria Isabel while negotiating the marriage. He'd been able to hammer out the details with her father instead. It was obviously much more practical to arrange these things on a man-to-man basis.

He wasn't quite sure when the idea of marriage had crystalized in his mind. He suspected the idea had begun to take shape even before he and Angie had left Mexico. There had been no doubt about the sensual attraction between them, and he had found her intelligent and charming. He'd also come to respect her courage and fortitude. A lot of women would have had hysterics after that scene with Ramon on the boat. Her connection to the Torres Dagger had injected a sense of fate into the equation. Somewhere along the line it had all begun to seem inevitable. At least to him.

In the distance he saw Angie come out of her cottage dressed in what looked like black jeans and a full-sleeved white shirt. She had a red windbreaker hooked over her shoulder. Her hair was bound neatly at the nape of her neck, and with a little imagination he could envision her as a nineteenth-century Torres woman about to take a morning ride. Even from this distance he could see the innate grace and pride in the way she moved.

Flynn turned and hurried into the bathroom to shower and shave. He wanted to catch up with her before she finished her walk on the beach.

Angie made her way down to the sand by following the twisting narrow path that wound its way between the tumbled rocks. It wasn't a particularly treacherous walk in daylight but you had to know where the path was. It tended to be obscured by the cliff outcrop and the clutter of rocks and small boulders. She used her hands to steady herself at several points along the way, stopping once or twice to examine an interesting chunk of driftwood.

When she finally reached the beach she stood for a moment at the water's edge, staring out to sea. Instinctively she sensed that Flynn would join her soon. He had found her down here the past two mornings, and she was quite certain he would look for her today, too. In spite of her ambivalent feelings toward him, she knew a part of her was anxious to see him.

Slowly she turned to pace along the sand. It was chilly, and after a few moments she opted to slip into the windbreaker. Fingers thrust into the back pockets of her jeans, she inhaled the crisp morning scent of the ocean and waited for Flynn to materialize nearby. The man moved as silently as a ghost, she reflected. She seldom heard him until he was next to her, especially down here on the beach where the sound of the waves masked smaller noises.

The strangely cautious manner he had been using around her for the past couple of days wouldn't last much longer, she sensed. She knew he had made a decision. But apparently he wasn't certain yet how to tell her about it. She had a hunch he'd talked to Julian, however. She'd seen the speculation in her uncle's eyes yesterday when she and Flynn had returned from the drive into Ventura. Had Julian wondered whether the subject had been brought out into the open during that drive?

She had been sorely tempted to satisfy her uncle's curiosity by loudly announcing that Flynn had not asked her to marry him while going to the grocery store. But she'd resisted the brief urge to make a joke out of it. It was hardly a joking matter.

That was the whole problem, she realized. She didn't quite know what to make of the unsettling situation. It was as though she were trapped in a fog with Flynn, unable to focus clearly and unable to escape entirely. She could hardly protest an offer of marriage when none had been made. But she was far too intuitive not to know that Flynn was shaping up his "grand destiny" and beginning to see her as part of it. What would she do when the time came to bring it all out into the open? Angie wasn't sure she knew just how she would react. That bothered her. It kept her awake at nights, and it made her behavior a bit unpredictable during the day. The only consolation was that she had a feeling both Uncle Julian and Flynn felt as if they were walking on eggshells.

Served them right.

"Angie?"

She whirled and found Flynn not more than a couple of feet away. He hadn't bothered with a jacket over his khaki shirt, and the breeze was playing with his short, carefully combed hair. He appeared to be oblivious to the chill as he watched her with the remote, faintly appraising expression that she was learning to recognize.

"Good morning, Flynn. Sleep well?"

"So polite," he murmured. "I slept as well as could be expected under the circumstances. How about you?"

She smiled. "Fine, thank you." She turned to resume her walk, and he fell into step beside her. "Any plans for the day?"

He said slowly, "I thought you might like to take a drive."

"To where?"

"Up to that horse ranch where the Challoner home once stood. I'd like to show it to you."

She thought about it. "All right."

Her answer satisfied him. Flynn seemed to relax a bit. "You know, I've done a lot of thinking about where to build a new home, Angie."

"Have you?"

"I want it designed from scratch to my specifications. I don't want to buy one that's already built." He flicked a glance at her profile as she walked beside him. "And I don't want it built with the quick, corner-cutting construction methods so many contractors use today."

Angie's mouth curved upward gently. "I understand. You want it built to last."

He nodded and shifted his gaze toward the horizon. "Yes. It needs to be the right kind of home, you see. A place where another generation can live."

"These days new generations tend to want to go their own way. They move to new states, find different careers than those their fathers have, build their own lives. And build their own homes. People don't think in terms of building a dynasty these days, Flynn."

"I know. People these days just live for the present. But things are going to be different with my family."

For a shattering instant the simple words went through Angie like a twist of lightning. Flynn Sangrey Challoner's family. She had a mental image of little dark-haired boys and girls running freely over rolling hills; playing in a garden that surrounded a built-for-the-ages home and clustering around their father's knee at night. For some reason the children were easy enough to visualize. It was when she tried to picture their mother that her mind refused to co-operate. With a sigh she gave up the project.

"Have you always been so certain of what you wanted, Flynn?" she asked quietly.

"For as long as I can remember. Ever since I heard the stories of my past and began to think about what had been lost." He slanted her a questioning look. "Didn't the tales you heard while growing up make you think about the past, Angie? Doesn't your uncle's interest in the family legends make you want to recreate what once existed?"

The idea never crossed my mind until I met you, Angie found herself thinking wistfully. *Now I don't seem to be able to stop thinking about it.* Aloud, she said carelessly, "I told you in Mexico that I'm definitely a woman of the present."

"We all live in the present, Angie," he said impatiently, "but that doesn't mean we can't link up with our pasts and build for the future. It's the way people used to view life, you know. In a lot of places in the world, they still do. We lose something vital when we lose our connection to the past."

"Are you hungry?"

His intent frown deepened. He obviously didn't care for the abrupt change of subject. "I suppose so. Sure. It's nearly seven thirty."

"I've got some eggs back at the cottage."

His expression cleared miraculously at the off-hand invitation. It was the first time she had invited him home for breakfast after one of their morning walks.

"Sounds great."

A little disconcerted by his grateful enthusiasm, Angie led the way toward her cottage.

Two hours later Angie stood beside Flynn on the crown of a rolling sweep of ground and watched a herd of Arabians graze on the spot where the Challoner homestead had once stood. Flynn surveyed the setting with an approving eye, one fist planted on his hip, his other arm resting on Angie's shoulders.

"You still have a view of the ocean from here, but you would be above the fog. And the house would have been protected from the wind. Ah, Angie, this is such good country. You can even forget Los Angeles is down the road. No wonder our families settled here."

Angie smiled, oddly aware of the beauty of the land. "I think I've always taken it for granted."

He glanced at her. "Taken what for granted?"

"The land. You're right, Flynn. This is beautiful country. Maybe you've developed more appreciation for it because you've had to spend so much time away from it. Or maybe your kind of love for the land is something that's born in a person."

"Maybe. I don't know. I just know that land like this should be valued."

"Where was the disputed piece of ground? The one the Torreses and the Challoners argued over?"

He moved his hand in a wide sweep. "Over there. From what I can tell it ran from that hillside down to the sea. Had a good year-round stream on it, which was one of the reasons both families needed it so badly. See? There's some livestock grazing near the water.''

Angie nodded. ''I see. And that stream was worth the price of a marriage?''

Flynn's arm tightened briefly on her shoulder, and for a moment she felt the strength in him through every fiber of her body.

''Oh, yes, Angie. It was worth the price.''

Perhaps it was, Angie found herself thinking. Standing here in the sunshine with Flynn's arm around her and the land stretched out before her, she could finally understand something of the tie that a man such as Flynn might feel for the land. A woman could feel that same connection, she realized. There was something vital, almost elemental about the sensation. For a moment Angie thought she could almost comprehend a marriage made for the reasons that first Challoner-Torres marriage had been contracted.

The realization disturbed her and she moved restlessly away from Flynn. The scent of the earth was strong today. It seemed to be affecting her reasoning processes.

''Angie?''

''Yes, Flynn?''

''I think I'd like my house to be built down there near the sea.'' He closed the small distance between them and pointed in the direction he wanted her to look. ''Maybe somewhere around that bluff on the point. Do you like that location? I know you like to be near the water.''

"That hunk of ground would be very expensive, Flynn."

"I know. But someday…"

She looked up at him with sudden emotion. "Someday, Flynn, I hope you get what you want."

He regarded her in silence for a moment, his gaze unreadable. "Thank you, Angie."

One afternoon at the end of the week, Julian walked into his study and found Angie filing some notes on handguns. He glanced around expectantly. "Here you are. Wondered where you'd disappeared. Where's Flynn?"

"He's driving into town to take some stuff to the post office."

"And you decided not to go with him?"

"I figured he doesn't really need me to hold his hand and show him how to buy stamps. He's a big boy."

Julian's brow lifted. "He's more than a boy, Angelina. He's a man. A good one. Aren't a lot of them around these days. Which probably explains why you haven't gotten married yet."

She looked up from where she was sitting in front of Julian's desk. "Starting to worry I'll stay a spinster all my life, Uncle Julian?"

He shook his head, lounging against the desk. "I'm not worried about that.…"

"Good, because you're hardly in a position to talk," she pointed out too sweetly. "You've never married, yourself."

His mouth crooked. "True. But you see, Angelina, dear, that only puts the entire weight of the burden on you.''

"What burden?''

"You owe it to yourself and to the families to make the right kind of marriage, Angelina. There's a future to be considered. And a past."

"I'm not a brood mare.''

He chuckled. "I was thinking more in terms of the cradle of future generations. Something along those lines.''

Angie burst out laughing. "That's very good, Uncle Julian. You may be ready to write something besides the Jake Savage stories.''

His eyes twinkled. "Why would I want to do that when those tales pay so damn well?''

"I see your point. Well, I suppose your poetic turn of phrase will just have to go unused. It's a cinch Jake Savage doesn't talk that way."

"And because he has a lot in common with Jake Savage, Flynn might not be able to put things so poetically, either. But, Angelina, that doesn't mean he doesn't think in those terms.''

Very slowly Angie put down the card she was filling out. "Don't tell me," she said very carefully, "that you have been delegated to broach the subject. I thought Flynn had more guts than to ask you to do it.''

Julian gave her a level stare. "What subject?''

"Marriage.''

"To Flynn?''

"Isn't that what we're discussing?'' she demanded.

"You're right, Angelina. If and when the time comes, Flynn will take care of matters himself. He knows damn good and well we're not living in the early 1800s. I don't have any authority over you in that respect."

"I'm so glad somebody realizes it. Lately I've had the oddest feeling I'm in the middle of a time warp." She tapped the card in her hand on the desk surface, her eyes on the ocean visible through the huge windows. "But he is going to ask, isn't he, Uncle Julian?"

"He's a good man, Angelina. Rock solid."

"He's an ex-mercenary. He's arrogant, ambitious and probably quite ruthless on occasion. He's got *plans.* Big plans. And he believes in things like the dagger. He wants to find a new Challoner dynasty, and I have a feeling he'd like to do it the way it was done originally."

"With a Torres bride?"

"Do you think I'm imagining things?"

"Nope." Julian straightened away from the desk and started toward the door. "You're a woman. I expect your intuition is probably fairly accurate. When he gets good and ready, he'll probably ask."

"I'll give him the same answer Maria Isabel gave Curtis Challoner!"

Julian grinned from the door. "Well, we all know what happened to her."

Unhappily Angie watched him go. She could not possibly agree to such an arrangement. Talk about being married for all the wrong reasons!

On the other hand, she wasn't sure she could bear

to let Flynn turn his back on her and walk out of her life in search of a more tractable bride. The very thought made her ache with a sense of loss that she didn't want to acknowledge.

She had fallen in love with Flynn. Angie no longer tried to fool herself on that score. It was the only explanation that made some sense out of this fog of uncertainty.

Another kind of fog rolled in that evening. This was the real kind that gathered out at sea and floated inland to shroud the coast. It had begun at sunset, and by the time Mrs. Akers had cleared the dinner dishes, it completely cloaked Julian's house.

The fire in the living room was cozy and comforting, Angie thought as she trailed in behind the men for the now-familiar sherry-hour routine. She was about to curl up in her usual position in an armchair while Julian and Flynn talked when she realized that something about tonight's routine would be different.

Flynn handed her a glass of sherry and remained standing in front of her. She looked up at him inquiringly.

"I'd like to talk to you." He was utterly calm, utterly controlled. The dark eyes were steady but unreadable.

Angie didn't need to be able to read those eyes. Her feminine intuition was screaming. The sherry in the glass she was holding slopped precariously for a moment before she managed to control it. A sudden sense of panic gripped her, and she looked helplessly across the room at Julian. Her uncle seemed totally oblivious. He'd already put on his reading glasses and was immersed in the newspaper.

"In your uncle's study, I think." Flynn reached down to take her hand.

Feeling trapped, Angie found herself letting him pull her gently to her feet. This was ridiculous. There was absolutely no reason to panic now that the moment was upon her. She was an adult, not a nineteen-year-old girl from another century. Hadn't she been expecting this for days? Now at least things would be put into words. No longer would she be forced to operate in this strange fog.

Silently she allowed herself to be towed along to Julian's study. En route she took two more sips from the sherry glass in her hand. She needed the fortification. This was it. Tonight she had to make the decision. And she still didn't know what that decision would be. *I'm not a brood mare,* she told herself on a wild little note of hysteria. *And I'm not the cradle of future generations of Challoners. I'm me, Angelina Morgan, and I've got my own plans for the future.*

Except that she didn't. Whatever plans she'd made for herself had evaporated when Flynn Challoner walked into her life.

Before she would work it all out, Flynn was releasing her hand, turning to close the door behind them. When he glanced at her she was standing stiffly in front of the cabinet that contained the Torres Dagger.

This was how she had felt nearly two hundred

years ago, Angie realized in stunned shock. This was exactly how she had felt; no, how *Maria Isabel* had felt. The same sense of panic, the same feeling of helplessness, the same outrage and the same passionate love for the man who was about to outline her future to her in no uncertain terms.

She backed another step and reached around to brace herself against the open cabinet. Her hand touched the case that contained the dagger. Damn it, she would not allow her imagination to take control like this.

"What did you want to talk about, Flynn?"

He stood in front of the door, solid and real and immovable. Well, she had wanted a solid enemy to fight, hadn't she?

"Angelina," he began in a more formal tone of voice than she had ever heard him use. "I want to discuss marriage."

"Flynn, I don't think—"

He ignored her small, breathless interruption. "I've been giving this a lot of thought, Angie."

"I was afraid of that."

"Angie, I'm serious. This is not a joke. Hear me out, please." It wasn't a request, it was an order. "You and I have more in common than most people have. We share a family history. We went through a lot together down in Mexico. That sort of experience builds a bond between people. We're attracted to each other on a physical basis, and on an intellectual basis I think we find each other interesting. We respect each other. In Mexico we talked easily right from the beginning. That hasn't changed. I'm not wealthy yet, but I can take care of you. Someday I'll be able to give you a great deal more. I'll build you a good home. And you have my word of honor, I'll be faithful. In short, I'll make you a good husband, Angie. I swear it.''

She stared at him, her pulse racing. Behind her back her nails were digging into the dagger case. ''Isn't this a little, uh, sudden, Flynn?'' It sounded weak, even to her own ears.

His head lifted with arrogant sureness. ''I know what I want, Angie. I'm very certain about what I'm doing.''

''Yes, you are, aren't you? You're always certain about what you're doing. You've got your whole damn life mapped out and nothing is going to get in the way of your goals. Well, I'm not at all sure I want to be included in those goals, Flynn Challoner. Thank you very much for considering me as your potential wife, but as it happens I've got a few plans of my own!''

''Angie, don't get upset.'' He took a step forward and halted abruptly when she immediately moved to the side a pace.

''What in hell do you mean by telling me not to get upset? What else do you expect me to do? I'm not Maria Isabel, Flynn. I'm Angie Morgan. And I don't really have the same ambitions that you do. I have no desire to be used to fulfill some family destiny only you can visualize.''

''Will you calm down and listen to me?'' Something flickered in his eyes. It might have been impatience or it might have been concern. ''You don't have to accept my offer of marriage tonight. I'm quite willing to give you a little time to think it over.''

''How generous of you!''

''Angie—''

''Why don't you be honest, at least, Flynn? It's not me you're offering to marry. It's the woman who can bring you the Torres Dagger. The woman you see as a link to your precious family past. The woman you think will make a good brood mare for the future. Well, I'll be damned if I'll be married for reasons such as that!''

''Stop it, Angie. You don't know what you're saying.''

''Don't I?'' She swung around and grabbed the dagger case. ''You think I don't know exactly where I fit in your scheme of things? I'm one step behind this stupid dagger and I know it.''

''That's not true. Angie, you're acting like a child. I sure as hell didn't expect you to get hysterical over this!''

''Shows how little you know me!'' she shot back furiously. ''You shouldn't go around offering marriage to someone you don't know very well, Flynn.'' She circled to the left, heading for the door. The dagger case was still clutched in her hand.

''Angie, come back here.''

''I'm going home to think over my fabulous offer of marriage. I plan to think it over for a very long time, Flynn. Well past my childbearing years.'' She swung around and opened the door.

''Angie, you little witch, come back here or so

help me—'' He broke off, striding through the door after her.

''Leave me alone, Flynn. And stop pretending that it's me you want. I know exactly what you want.''

''You don't know what you're saying.''

''Shall I prove it? I can, you know.'' Head high, she challenged him with furious, frantic eyes.

''Angie, I'm going to lose my temper,'' he warned softly.

''I've already lost mine!'' She whirled and fled through the living room, not even glancing at Julian, who was looking startled by the unexpected scene taking place before his eyes.

''Angie!''

She paid no attention, racing through the door and out into the fog-shrouded night. Behind her she heard Flynn. He would catch up with her soon. She didn't stand a chance of outrunning him. She sucked in a breath of chilled air and dashed for the edge of the bluff overlooking the sea.

She couldn't make out the water below but she could hear it foaming and crashing against the bottom of the cliff. The tide was in, and occasionally a splash of white was visible through the fog. Frantically she opened the dagger case. Flynn was running silently. He would materialize behind her at any second.

The dagger slid easily into the wide sleeve of her yellow shirt. She snapped the case shut just as Flynn appeared. He came gliding out of the fog, his harsh face barely discernible in the swirling shadows.

"Just what the hell do you think you're doing?" he bit out.

"Proving a point!"

"What point? That I don't want you? That's idiotic and you know it. Don't you remember that night in L.A.?"

"You only care about the history around me, and I swear I won't be married for historical purposes!"

"Angie, I'm not asking you to marry me just because of the past!"

"Yes, you are and I'll prove it!" Without a second's hesitation she tossed the empty dagger case over the edge of the cliff. It sailed out into the fog and disappeared. A moment later the waves closed over it. Angie turned back to confront Flynn. "Okay, Challoner. The dagger's gone. Still want to marry me?"

Eight

Time hung suspended, trapped in the light, swirling fog. For a shattering moment Angie was no longer certain of the era in which she lived. A part of her was suddenly aware that Maria Isabel had once precipitated similar confrontations with Curtis Challoner. Nothing seemed to have changed, most especially not the risks. The sea pulsed rhythmically at the base of the cliff, and the faint light from the house shone erratically through the mist. Flynn stood utterly still, staring into the foaming darkness where the dagger case had disappeared.

Angie was cold with a chill that had nothing to do with the damp night air. She was vaguely aware that her fingers were shaking. Soon her whole body would be shivering. She wished she could see Flynn's expression, but simultaneously she dreaded the moment when he would turn to face her. Instinct warned her to turn and run. Pride and a strange disorientation kept her where she was. The length of the dagger felt hard and frozen on the warmth of her skin. She should remove it from her sleeve, show it to Flynn and end this unreal scene. But she couldn't seem to move.

"Flynn?" His name was a ragged, husky sound in her throat. Angie wasn't even certain he had heard.

"Do you hate me so much, then, Angie?"

Slowly he turned to look at her and the fog-reflected glow of the house lights fell on his stark, harsh features. Angie registered the combination of shock, fury and pain in the shadows of his eyes, and she felt abruptly dizzy.

"Flynn, I don't...I didn't..." The words tripped and fell over themselves as she struggled to regain a sense of equilibrium. Unconsciously she put out a hand as if to ward him off although he had made no move to touch her.

"I knew you weren't exactly head over heels in love with me, but I didn't realize—" He broke off, shaking his head once in bleak despair. "I didn't think you would throw a couple of hundred years of our history into the sea just to make your point. What have I done to make you want this kind of revenge?"

Angie shook off the numbing disorientation. "Nothing, Flynn. Nothing at all. You saved both the dagger and me down in Mexico, and you didn't steal it when you could have done so easily. You've offered me what must seem to you a reasonable, honorable marriage alliance. You've behaved like a gentleman, and instead of returning the courtesy I lost my self-control entirely. There is absolutely no excuse for the way I acted. After all, it's not as if I'm a headstrong nineteen-year-old at the mercy of the men who ran her life. Maria Isabel had a right to fight back any way she could. She had no option.''

He came forward, gliding soundlessly through the mist until he was only a step away from her.

''Angie—''

''I'm sorry, Flynn. Unlike Maria Isabel, I do have an option. All I have to say is no.'' With fumbling fingers she extracted the dagger from her sleeve and held it out to him. ''I wanted to make a point, but as you said, I wouldn't throw away a couple of hundred years of history to do it.'' *Not when that history means so much to you,* she added silently.

Flynn stared at the dagger before slowly reaching out to take it from her. She could read nothing in his face now; not even relief. That was preferable to the unmistakable fury and anguish she had seen a moment earlier. Without waiting for his response Angie turned and ran back toward the lights of her uncle's house.

At the door she changed her mind about going inside. The idea of facing Uncle Julian was sufficiently daunting to send her around to the driveway. Flynn had the keys to her car, but she kept a spare taped inside the glove compartment. Angie opened the car door, slipped into the driver's seat and dug out the extra key.

All she wanted right now was to be alone. Twisting the key in the ignition, Angie put the Toyota in gear. Gravel crunched under the wheels as she pulled out of the drive. Her startling burst of temper was firmly back under control. In fact, most of it seemed to have been replaced by a sense of shock at her own behavior.

She had known Flynn's proposal was coming. Her intuition had told her to expect it. Angie chased the car's headlights into the fog and asked herself over and over again why she had responded so violently. She wasn't Maria Isabel. She wasn't trapped the way the other woman had been.

But as often as she repeated that to herself, Angie couldn't argue with the inner conviction that she wasn't really free. To be truly free she would have to feel nothing more than casual friendship for Flynn. And heaven knew that what she felt went far beyond friendship. She was in love with the man.

Maybe that was the same trap in which Maria Isabel had found herself, Angie realized with sudden insight. Perhaps the other woman had been caught not only in the cage of the social structure in which she lived but in the snare of her growing passion for Curtis Challoner. The pressure of being forced into a marriage in which the groom was primarily interested in the settling of a land dispute would be bad enough, but to be in love with him and aware that your love was not returned would be infinitely worse. The first situation could conceivably be viewed philosophically. The second would mean anguish.

And it was the second scenario in which she

found herself, Angie thought as she parked her car in front of her cottage. But her anguish had not given her the right to pull that stupid stunt with the dagger. Well, one thing was for certain. After tonight she wouldn't have to worry about dealing with a proposal of marriage from Flynn. She'd seen the expression in his eyes when he'd turned to look at her after she'd thrown the dagger case into the sea. No man who looked at a woman in that way was likely to renew his proposal.

Letting herself inside the cozy little cottage, Angie switched on the hall light and tossed the Toyota key onto a nearby table. She stood trying to decide what to do next.

Aimlessly she wandered into the living room and considered starting a fire. The chill she had felt on the cliffs still seemed to be eating at her. Building a blaze seemed to require too much effort, however, so Angie settled for turning up the thermostat and going out into the kitchen to pour herself a snifter of sherry. She was on her way back into the living room, sherry in hand, when she heard her uncle's Mercedes approaching.

It would be Flynn. Instinct told her that with nerve-shattering clarity. Angie stood riveted to the hall floor, the glass clutched in her fingers, and listened as the car's engine died. A second later the door slammed shut, and then there was a soundless interval as Flynn moved silently up the path to her front door. When the peremptory knock came she almost dropped the sherry onto the tile floor.

"Angie, open the door." Flynn didn't knock a second time. His voice was filled with command.

She could refuse to open the door, Angie thought distractedly. Would he force his way inside? "What do you want, Flynn?"

"You and I have a few things to talk about."

"I think…" She paused, moistening her lower lip. "I think it would be better if the discussion waited until morning."

"Open the door, Angie, or I'll find my own way into the house."

It wasn't a threat; simply a statement of fact. She didn't doubt for a moment that he could and would do it. Unsteadily Angie went to the door and slowly opened it. Flynn stood on the front step, harshly revealed in the light of the outside lamp. The dagger was held loosely in his left hand, the stones in its handle gleaming dully in the yellow porch light. His dark eyes moved over her and then went to her glass. He stepped purposefully into the hall.

"Why don't you pour me a glass of whatever that is. I could use it." Without waiting for her acknowledgment Flynn strode into the small living room and glanced around. Then he went over to the fireplace and picked up one of the store-bought fire logs that lay on the hearth. "I don't know why you don't buy real wood instead of this compressed sawdust."

Angie stared at his back as he set the dagger on an end table and went down on one knee to strike a match. "I buy those logs because they're so much simpler to use. Flynn, why are you complaining about my instant fire logs? No one asked you to build a fire in the first place.''

"I'm aware of that. You haven't asked me for a damn thing since we got back from Mexico, have you?'' He finished setting the log alight and remained crouched where he was, gazing fiercely into the flames.

"I don't understand what you're trying to say.''

"Go pour me a drink, Angie.'' He ran his fingers wearily through his hair and got to his feet.

Nervously, feeling as if her emotions were dangling above the point of the dagger that had caused all the trouble, Angie did as she was told. When she returned to the living room with a second glass, she found Flynn sprawled in a chair. He was gazing broodingly into the fire, but he looked up briefly as she handed him the sherry.

"Thanks.'' He took a deep swallow. "Good Spanish sherry. Sort of fits the occasion, doesn't it?''

"What occasion?'' Gingerly Angie took a seat on the other side of the fireplace. She decided she didn't want to hear the answer and rushed on to add, "Flynn, I'm sorry. I know that was a stupid trick I pulled out there on the cliffs. I don't know what got into me. I've never done anything like that before in my life.''

He sighed and stretched his legs out closer to the blaze. "You're a female and you're a Torres. I should have expected the fireworks.''

Some of Angie's contriteness evaporated. "That's an asinine explanation of my behavior. Oversimplified, illogical and chauvinistic.''

He wasn't listening. Apparently Flynn was trying to sort something out in his mind. His brow furrowed. "It's just that for the past several days you've seemed so quiet, so reasonable, so…" He paused, searching for the word. "So amenable. I thought you understood. I was under the impression that you were feeling cooperative about the idea of rejoining the two families."

"That's how you see it, isn't it? A way of reliving the past."

His gaze flickered toward her briefly, and then he looked back at the fire. "No, Angie. That's not the way I see it. No one relives the past. You *build* on the past. Can't you understand the distinction?"

"No, but I'm beginning to think you do understand it." She took a sip of sherry. "The past means a lot to you."

"What does it mean to you, Angie? Nothing at all?"

She shook her head. "No, it's beginning to have meaning. More than I want it to have."

He frowned at her. "Why do you say that?"

"The past is starting to make me edgy, Flynn. I find it a little frightening, if you want to know the truth. Before I met you the tale of Maria Isabel Torres and Curtis Challoner was just that: a tale. Interesting on some levels, amusing on others. But essentially nothing more than a legend."

"What are you saying? That it's becoming more than a legend?"

"In some ways."

Relief flared in his gaze. "But, Angie, that's

good. That's the way it should be. You should feel the past in your bones. It should be a part of you, a touchstone, a foundation. It deserves to be more than just a collection of stories.''

She tilted her head to one side, studying him. ''I didn't say it was becoming any of those things. I said I found it a bit frightening.''

''Maybe for you that's the first step to having it become real.''

''Flynn, if that's the first step, I'm not exactly anxious to take the next step. Damn it, why are you acting so pleased? I'm the person who just put you through hell by letting you think I'd thrown your precious dagger into the ocean! I should think you'd be furious.''

''It wasn't my dagger you pulled that stunt with, it was *our* dagger and I *was* furious. I couldn't believe you'd do something like that just out of spite.''

''It was hardly spite that made me do it!'' She was starting to overreact again, Angie thought wildly. What was the matter with her? A few minutes ago she was feeling apologetic and extremely guilty for having behaved in such a juvenile manner. Now the resentment was starting to flare to life again. Her emotions seesawed as they hovered over the imagined point of the dagger.

A small smile briefly edged Flynn's mouth. His eyes warmed suddenly. ''No, it wasn't spite, was it? You were enraged. There's a difference. I'll bet Maria Isabel looked a lot like you looked when she lost her temper with my ancestor. All fire and fury and passion. I really should have been expecting it. After all, I know something about the passion buried in you. But I was off guard. You'd fooled me into thinking you were going to be very twentieth century about my marriage proposal. A polite yes or no was the response I anticipated. And to tell you the truth, I was expecting a yes.''

''Flynn, I think this has gone far enough. You're obviously determined to pretend I'm another Maria Isabel. I'm not. For one thing, I'm several years older than she was when she was forced into marriage. For another I am a child of the twentieth century. You're absolutely right. All I have to give you is a simple yes or no. Frankly, though, I'm surprised the offer is still open.''

''Because of what you did back there on the cliffs?'' He looked at her quizzically. ''That doesn't change anything, Angie.''

''Really? What would you have done if I'd actually thrown that dagger into the sea?''

''Calm down,'' he soothed. ''You didn't throw it into the ocean. Therefore we don't have to discuss alternatives.''

Restlessly Angie got to her feet and put her sherry glass down on a table. She stood leaning against the mantel and stared down into the fire. ''I want to know what you would have done, Flynn.''

''Why?''

''I guess because I'm trying to figure out exactly how much that dagger means to you. Would you still be offering to marry me if I'd thrown that damn thing into the sea?''

''Yes.''

She looked up, her eyes wide and searching. "Wouldn't you have hated me?"

"No, but I would have been a little worried that you hated me." He got to his feet and came to stand in front of her. "But you don't hate me, do you Angie?"

She caught her breath. "No."

He nodded. "Thank God for that. Your temper I can handle. Your hatred would be something else again."

"You've convinced yourself that's all my scene on the cliffs amounts to, haven't you? A display of feminine temper."

"And passion." He lifted a hand to stroke the line of her throat up to her chin. Gently he tipped her face upward. "You took me by surprise. But maybe that's because I'd let myself be lulled into believing I knew what you were thinking. The truth is I didn't know what you were really thinking. I made some assumptions that were obviously wrong. I suppose you could say I deserved that scene on the cliffs. But, Angie, you haven't been exactly communicative lately. Ever since we left L.A. you've been withdrawn."

"And you haven't quite known why, have you?" She searched his eyes.

"I thought at first it was because you were hurt by the fact that I'd kept my identity from you down in Mexico. But you seemed to get over that. You've been friendly enough this past week, just distant. This would have been so much simpler if we really were living in the past. Then I could have negotiated the marriage with Julian. I wouldn't have had to second-guess you or try to figure out what you were thinking. What have you been thinking, Angie? Why did you explode tonight?''

She watched him, feeling helpless to explain. Any man who longed for the times when a marriage alliance could be negotiated between two males was probably incapable of understanding how she had felt this evening.

''Flynn, I once told you that when I married it wouldn't be for business reasons. Do you remember?''

He inclined his head warily. ''As I recall you said you would marry for love and passion.''

''I haven't changed my mind.''

He bent his head and brushed his mouth lightly against her own. Then, without lifting his lips from hers, he whispered, ''How can you say there isn't passion between us?''

Angie shivered. She couldn't bring herself to move out of reach although Flynn held her in place with only the tip of his finger and the promise of his mouth. ''I haven't said there isn't passion, Flynn. But there does seem to be a lack of love.''

''Love will follow, sweetheart. Just as it followed for Maria Isabel.'' He kissed her again, slowly, his hand moving to cradle the nape of her neck. His fingers began toying with the pins that held her coiled hair. ''Give it a chance, Angie. You want me. I've known that from the beginning. And we have so much in common, so much to build on together.

I'll take care of you, honey. I swear it. Just give me a chance.''

She closed her eyes as his lips traced a path along the line of her jaw up to her earlobe. Angie could feel the sensual tension beginning to vibrate in him, striking a chord within herself that responded eagerly.

''What about you, Flynn? Do you think that in time you'll fall in love with me?''

''Sweetheart, love is a word for women like you and Maria Isabel to use to label passion and commitment. I can use it, too, if that's what you want. But it doesn't mean much to me, not when I compare it to what I know I already feel for you.''

''And what is that, Flynn?''

He tugged free one of the pins that held her hair. It fell soundlessly to the carpet. ''Desire, for one thing. I've never wanted a woman the way I want you.'' His fingers found another pin and tugged it loose. It, too, dropped to the floor. ''A sense of protectiveness. I want to take care of you, Angie.'' A third pin followed the other two. ''A feeling of rightness. A feeling that we belong together.'' Two more pins were eased out of her dark, tawny hair. ''A sense of a shared past. And a sense of the future.'' Her hair tumbled free and spilled over his hand. He curled his fingers deeply into it and used it to gently hold her still for his kiss.

Angie's arms wound about his neck as her mouth opened for him. Her precariously balanced emotions were being pushed unmercifully in the direction Flynn wanted them to go. She knew it, recognized that she was allowing her love for him to overwhelm her logic, but in that moment she didn't want to take the necessary step back that would salvage the situation. The dagger's blade was as tempting as it was dangerous.

"Flynn…"

"I think that what happened tonight was my own fault, Angie." He whispered huskily into her mouth. "I never should have let you put so much distance between us. I should have kept you close, the way you were in Mexico. The way you were that night in the hotel in L.A. Instead I tried to give you time to adjust. That was a mistake."

"No, Flynn. It wasn't a mistake. I do need time to think."

"Come to bed with me, sweetheart, and afterward tell me where your thinking is going to lead you."

She heard the certainty in his words. "You're so sure of yourself, aren't you?"

"Angie, I know what's right for us. I can feel it, damn it!" His hands tightened on her abruptly, pulling her into the warmth of his body.

The flames from the hearth shimmered and flared as Angie surrendered to Flynn's heat. She loved him and she wanted him with all her being. The issues between them were still unresolved but she could not deny herself this chance to be with him again. All the mounting tension of the past several days seemed to be culminating tonight, first in anger and now in passion.

"Come with me, sweetheart. I'll show you that what we have is right." Flynn picked her up, cradling her in his arms as he started down the hall to her bedroom.

Angie silently abandoned herself to the smoldering flames of her love. She clung to him, head nestled on his shoulder as he carried her into the bedroom. The mounting desire in Flynn was a pulsating force that was as strong and relentless as the sea outside. It charged the atmosphere in the darkened room, and Angie was tinglingly aware of it as he let her slide slowly down the length of his body.

When she found her feet she realized that her sense of balance was off. Her fingers splayed across his shoulders as she sought to steady herself.

"Don't worry, sweetheart. I'll hold you. I'll take care of you." The words were dark, seductive caresses, every bit as effective as his touch.

"We should talk, Flynn...."

"We've talked enough. We've done too much talking. I should have been taking you to bed every night this past week instead of trying to give you time. I wasn't cut out to be a gentleman with you."

He undid the buttons of her shirt, sliding the garment off and letting it drop to the floor. Her hair flowed around her shoulders as his palms dropped to cup her bare breasts.

"Finding you at the same time I found the dagger was fate, Angie. It had to be. How can you even question it?"

She didn't try to answer that. There was, after all, no logical response to such a statement, especially not when your body was agreeing with every word. Angie shivered with impending excitement as Flynn rubbed his thumbs gently across her hardening nipples. Then she reached out with a passionate aggression of which she was only vaguely aware and began to undress him.

"Yes," he groaned hoarsely. "Show me, honey. Show me that you want me. Prove it to both of us."

She fumbled with the buttons of his shirt until, frustrated as much as she was by her ineffectual efforts, Flynn smiled a little and stepped back. He finished unfastening his clothing, discarding his moccasins, the shirt, the twill pants with quick, impatient movements. Then, standing in front of her in only his briefs, he went back to removing Angie's clothes. This task he performed with infinitely more patience than he had just exhibited with his own clothes. It was obvious he took pleasure in the process.

Angie ran her hands down his chest, an aching sensation stirring deep in her body. "You're so hard," she murmured, flexing her nails lightly into his skin.

"I know." He sounded wryly amused by the fact. "I can hardly hide it, can I?" Deliberately he cupped her buttocks in his hands and pressed his hips against her.

She flushed at the unyielding thrust of his body. "I...I didn't mean that way. I meant all over. Physically, emotionally, the way you think. You're a hard man, Flynn Challoner." She put her lips to his shoulder and tasted him with the tip of her tongue. When he responded with muttered words of desire, she let him feel the edge of her teeth.

"Little cat. I'm going to enjoy returning the favor." He released her briefly to pull back the sheet and the comforter on her bed and then he scooped her up and set her down in the middle. A moment later he followed, his body sprawling heavily along hers as he pulled her into his arms.

Angie welcomed the heat and weight of him, twining her legs with his and sinking her fingers into his hair. She sighed his name as she felt his hand gliding over her skin. He touched her with increasing intimacy while the fire between them flamed into full life. His fingers found the exquisitely sensitive skin on the inside of her thigh and then prowled closer to the dampening heart of her desire. She arced her breast against his mouth when he made good his passionate threat and trapped a nipple between his teeth.

There in the darkness Angie was able to put aside the logic and uncertainty that made her balk at the idea of marriage. There in the shadows of the bedroom she was free to glory in the passionate excitement only Flynn could arouse in her. In the morning she would deal with reality. Tonight all that mattered was losing herself in Flynn's arms.

"Angie, you don't ever have to be afraid of me. You're mine, and I'll take care of what belongs to me." He rolled onto his back, drawing her with him until she was lying on top. Then he stroked his hands down her back to the curve of her hips. "Now, honey, *now* I want to feel you all over me. I need to be inside. You're so warm and wet and clinging inside...."

Angie gasped as he eased her down toward his waiting hardness. The images she'd had all evening of being poised above the dagger suddenly crystalized into an unexpected version of reality.

She had no more time to think about it. Flynn's fingers were digging luxuriously into her thighs, and he held her still as he thrust upward.

"Yes, sweetheart, oh, God, *yes!*"

Angie clung to him, her body adjusting to the beloved invasion. Flynn anchored her fiercely as he lifted his hips against her softness. His mouth found hers, drinking deeply, and she felt the strength of his hands as he guided her into the rhythm he wanted.

Deep within her tendrils of delicious, aching tension spun slowly outward and then began to coalesce. She was aware of the slickness of perspiration on Flynn's chest, knew the passionate firmness of him as he buried himself within her, felt the unbreakable hold in which she was held. Suddenly the tension broke, washing over her while she shivered in its wake. Before she had even begun to recover she heard Flynn's harsh cry of satisfaction and triumph and then he was shuddering in savage release. His hold on her didn't slacken as he followed her into the temporary oblivion.

Angie came awake slowly the next morning; calmly, clearly aware of what she was going to do. She had known it all along, she realized. That was why she had experienced the frightening sensation of being trapped. She stretched and turned on her side. The bed was empty.

Pushing back the covers, she climbed out of bed, pausing briefly to let a few sore muscles adjust to the new position. She listened attentively for a moment but heard no telltale sounds from the kitchen. Intuition told her that Flynn had gone done to the beach. Either that, she thought wryly as she glanced around the room, or he had gone back to the hacienda. Either way, they were going to have to come to an understanding about this sort of behavior.

She pulled on a pair of jeans and a vivid red oversize top that fell below her waist. She belted the shirt with a wide snakeskin tie. Then Angie located a pair of shoes and her windbreaker. She didn't bother to put her hair into its usual twist. The first priority was to find Flynn.

He wasn't hard to locate. She saw him as soon as she reached the top of the cliff overlooking the beach. He was standing at the water's edge, gazing out to sea. Angie knew a wave of anguished panic. Perhaps he had changed his mind, after all. Perhaps he was down there trying to figure out how to tell her he was withdrawing his proposal of marriage.

The flash of doubt sent her hurrying forward, scrambling down the narrow path to the beach. She didn't think he could have heard her over the sound of the surf but something made him turn and watch as she walked toward him through the sand. The unreadable expression on his lean face almost caused her to lose her nerve.

''Challoner,'' she began, struggling to find refuge in flippancy, ''there's something we have to get cleared up about your poor morning-after etiquette.''

"Is there?"

He wasn't going to make this easy for her, Angie thought, dismayed. And the flippancy didn't seem to be working too well, either. "You're not supposed to just disappear from the bed the way you do. You're supposed to stick around and make warm, meaningful conversation. Or at least make coffee."

He stared at her. "I see. Did you have something warm and meaningful you wanted to say?"

She flinched but held on to her nerve. "Yes, as a matter of fact, I did."

Wariness and hope flared in his eyes. He controlled both emotions almost immediately. "And what would that be?"

"I've decided to accept your proposal of marriage." Angie took refuge now in formality. "That is, if it's still open." She held her breath.

"Why?"

The stark question was the last thing she had been expecting. Uneasily she tried to concentrate. "For all the reasons you suggested. We're compatible, we have some history in common. You're a good man, a strong man, not a playboy. I think I can trust you. And maybe there is a certain sense of fate involved. I don't know about that last part. I don't think I want to know about it." Then in silence she added the real reason, *because I love you, Flynn Sangrey Challoner.* She waited.

He studied her for a long moment, the crisp, cool wind whipping his shirt and ruffling his hair. Behind him the sea lapped almost to his moccasins. Angie felt the bite of the morning breeze. The cold seemed to go right through her.

"All right," Flynn said finally.

She smiled tremulously. "Is that all you can say? All right?"

He hesitated and then a hint of a smile touched his mouth. "How about, 'thank you and I promise not to vacate the bed in future without telling you where I'm going'?"

"That's better." She held out her hand, and after a couple of seconds he took it, his fingers closing warmly and a little fiercely around hers.

"Angie?"

"Hmm?" She caught her hair and held it out of her eyes.

"I'll make it work. I'll make it all right."

Not understanding what he meant, she wrinkled her nose and smiled up at him. "I don't doubt it for a moment."

Nine

Three days later Angie furtively sought refuge in her uncle's study. A quick glance around the room revealed she had the place to herself, and with a deep sigh of relief she shut the door and collapsed into the nearest chair.

She should have guessed that once Flynn had her agreement to the marriage, there would be no stopping him until the wedding had taken place. He had taken charge completely, and she had felt like a leaf caught up in a whirlwind. She had also felt quite unnecessary. Flynn was organizing everything from the flowers right down to the plane tickets for her mother.

Occasionally she was consulted, but Angie had the distinct impression it was more out of politeness than because Flynn actually wanted her opinion. Mrs. Akers was getting the brunt of Flynn's attention this morning, however, as he went over the reception menu with her. Angie had gratefully slipped out of his path, fleeing to the study on the hunch that Flynn wouldn't think to look for her there. If he missed her, he would probably assume she was taking a walk on the beach. Craftily, she had mentioned the idea earlier at breakfast.

Breakfast had been at her cottage this morning, just as it had for the past several mornings, but not because Flynn had spent the night. He hadn't. In fact, he hadn't spent any night with her since the scene with the dagger. She wasn't quite sure how to interpret that, but she suspected it had something to do with his grim determination to do things *right*.

The door opened and Angie jumped. She relaxed as Julian walked into the room. He smiled as she sank back into the chair.

"I figured you might be hiding in here. Picked up an extra cup of coffee for you from the kitchen. Mrs. Akers and Flynn never even noticed me."

"Too busy trying to decide between shrimp puffs and salmon canapes probably." Gratefully Angie accepted the coffee. She grinned wryly at her uncle as he sat down in his swivel desk chair. "Honestly, Uncle Julian, I knew he was basically a take-charge personality. I saw enough of them when I was in personnel work to recognize the type. But I never thought he'd apply his talents in quite this manner. I've always heard weddings are women's business. All the groom has to do is show up on time."

Julian shrugged. "He wants it done right."

"So he'll do it himself."

"Don't forget he also wants it done quickly. Only two weeks from today. Given the tight schedule he probably figures he'd better stay in command."

"He's like a general on a battlefield. Every time he spots me he gives me another set of orders. And Mrs. Akers appears to have been placed second in command."

"This wedding is important to him," Julian said gently. "He's not taking charge this way because he's a natural-born social butterfly!"

In spite of herself Angie laughed at the image. "A butterfly in moccasins. I like that. No, I agree. He's about as much a social butterfly as Jake Savage is."

Julian ignored her. "You have to understand, Angelina. Rituals and traditions are bound to be important to a man who's intent on rebuilding a family. And the wedding that forms the basis of his new…"

"Dynasty?" Angie suggested dryly when her uncle stopped to fish for an appropriate word.

"Well, that's putting it a bit dramatically, I think. But your marriage is a foundation on which Flynn intends to build. He wants it started properly."

Angie smiled gently. "I understand, Uncle Julian. It's just that at times it's a little nerve-racking. Maybe I've got bridal jitters."

Julian studied her. "Are you really nervous about this marriage? There's absolutely no need, you know. Flynn will make you an excellent husband."

"The question is, will I make him the right kind of wife?" She tilted her head back against the chair cushion. "He's so set on reestablishing the Challoner-Torres line. He has an image in his head, a goal that only he can see. I'm not marrying him because I'm equally committed to founding a dynasty."

"Why are you marrying him, then?"

She closed her eyes briefly. "For the usual reasons."

"The usual reasons?" Her uncle arched one brow. "It can't be for money. Flynn's cash is tied up in land and likely to remain that way for some time to come. Every extra cent he gets for the next few years will be funneled back into property, I think. You'll have what you need and a few luxuries, but you won't be driving a Ferrari. Let's see, what other 'usual reasons' are there? How about social status? Nope, we have to assume it's not for that. Right now the Challoners and the Torreses have virtually no social status. That may change someday, but it will be a long time in the future. Desperation? You see thirty on the horizon and are starting to panic? I don't think so. You've always seemed amazingly content with yourself and your independence. So much so that I was beginning to think you never would marry. And if you had been panicking, I think you would have had some marriage candidates lined up before you went to Mexico. That leaves us with one other possibility. You're in love with him, aren't you?"

Angie looked at her uncle through eyes narrowed half in amused resignation and half in irritation. "As I said, I'm marrying for the usual reasons."

"He needs your love, Angelina. Any man who is

as intent on his goals as Flynn is will desperately need a woman's love during the coming years. The drive and the ambition will eat him alive, otherwise.''

Angie thought about that. He seems so strong, Uncle Julian.''

"He is strong. It takes a hell of a strong man to set his kind of goals and then commit himself to the work it will take to meet them. But that kind of energy and drive can destroy even the strongest people. The effort will take a lot out of him and without a softer side in his life...well, I shouldn't have to tell you, Angelina. You're the expert in personnel work. You must have seen what can happen.''

She nodded. "I've seen it. Strong, committed people can build their own traps. And you're right. Energy and ambition can swallow a man whole. And in Flynn's case there's the added factor of what he's already done in his life just to get to where he is now. It's strange, Uncle Julian, but I've never thought of Flynn in the same objective terms I'm accustomed to applying to others.''

"I'd hardly call that strange.'' Julian smiled affectionately. "People seldom are objective about the people they love.''

Angie considered where that logic led. Flynn seemed quite objective about her, she reflected. He knew exactly why he was marrying her; had all the reasons lined up in a neat, orderly row. It followed that he didn't love her, but it didn't necessarily mean he couldn't learn to love her.

With an exclamation of frustration, Angie set

down her coffee cup. There was no sense tearing
herself apart trying to figure out Flynn's actions. He
was a law unto himself, just as Curtis Challoner and
the head of the neighboring Torres family had been
laws unto themselves nearly two hundred years ago.
Uncle Julian was right; it took that kind of man to
build a dynasty. And maybe, just maybe you could
argue, as Julian had, that such a man needed love
to maintain a healthy balance in his life.

But what of the woman who committed herself to
giving that love? What did she need in return in
order to survive emotionally? Angie stirred restlessly, drawing her legs up under her as she sat in
the chair. She would receive a great deal from Flynn
Challoner. He was honorable in his own way. He
had his own code, but he lived by it and he could
be trusted. There would be passion and honor and
commitment. Why on earth was she feeling uneasy?
Many women got a lot less out of the marriage contract.

Something stirred in her mind, a faint whisper of
another voice from another time. It could have been
Maria Isabel but of course it wasn't, Angie told herself. It was simply her own growing affinity for the
woman who had married Curtis Challoner. Somehow Angie knew, though, that a lot of the thoughts
going through her head lately were hardly original.
Maria Isabel had given herself the same lectures;
asked herself the same questions. And wound up
with the same sense of frustration.

"Angie! Angie, where the hell are you?" Flynn's
voice sounded loudly from the hall. A moment later

the study door was flung open. "There you are. I've been looking all over for you." He nodded briefly at Julian, who smiled serenely in return, and then strode toward Angie. He had a list in his hand that was covered with his distinctive scrawl. "Do you want tomato-basil sandwiches or smoked salmon?"

"Gee, that's a tough choice, Flynn."

He frowned at her. "This is not a joke, Angie. I'm very serious. Mrs. Akers says they'll both be on the salty side and that we should probably choose one or the other. We couldn't make up our minds so I thought I'd see if you had an opinion."

"Caviar," Angie said succinctly.

"What?"

"How about caviar if you want something salty? Think how impressed the guests will be."

His face cleared. "You're absolutely right. We'll set a big bowl of caviar on an ice block and surround it with little crackers and things." He started for the door and then halted as he caught sight of Julian again. "Speaking of the guests, did you make out that list?"

"I've got it ready."

"Good. Angie can add your list to hers and address the invitations this afternoon. I want them in the mail by five o'clock. It's short enough notice as it is."

"Don't worry, Flynn," Julian advised. "Everyone on my list will show up."

Flynn nodded in satisfaction. "Good." He vanished out the door.

Angie eyed her uncle. "We're providing all the guests?"

Julian smiled wryly. "Well, Flynn doesn't have any friends in this area. And I got the feeling that the few friends he does have are scattered around the globe. By the time the invitations reached them the wedding would be over."

"I wonder if that bothers him," Angie mused.

"I doubt it. He just wants people there. I don't think he's particularly fussy about which people."

"Then why invite anyone at all? Why not keep this thing just family?"

"Angie, you don't understand. Guests are important to a wedding such as this. They're witnesses. The more witnesses the better as far as Flynn is concerned."

"Part of the foundation process, I guess." Angie levered herself to her feet. "Well, I've received my orders of the day. Fat lot of good it did trying to hide. I think I'd better go start addressing invitations. You're sure your friends will come?"

"Are you kidding? They'll be dying of curiosity. I've told them that my niece is marrying the real Jake Savage?"

"Uncle Julian!"

"That's not all. I decided Flynn was forgetting about one of the most important prewedding customs, so I took care to remedy the matter."

"What custom?"

"A surprise bachelor party for the groom. I've invited a selected handful of male friends."

"I'm not sure I want to hear the rest of this. You're planning a surprise party?"

"Yup. But it will have to be a few days before the wedding instead of the night before because your mother will be arriving the day before the ceremony. She'll be staying here, and it would be a bit awkward trying to surprise Flynn with your mother in the house."

Angie grinned. "Probably not a good idea for the mother of the bride to see the groom in a drunken stupor the night before he marries her daughter."

"I can't imagine Flynn in a drunken stupor."

"Neither can I. Should be interesting. One thing, though, Uncle Julian. I want you to promise me that there won't be any nude girls leaping out of cakes!"

"You're starting to sound wifely already."

A week later Flynn went down to the beach by himself to think about the expense involved in ordering the brand of champagne he wanted. When the caviar had been added to the already lengthy list of hors d'oeuvres, a considerable dent had been put into the budget.

Ah, well, he told himself. The budget was a loose one. He could worry about economizing after the wedding. He'd go ahead and order the real stuff, French champagne instead of the domestic variety.

The decision made, he halted at the water's edge and wondered why he was still feeling faintly uneasy. It couldn't be worry about the wedding, itself. Everything was going perfectly. Responses were already coming back from the invitations. Mrs. Akers seemed to have the food preparation under control. The minister had confirmed the time and day.

He scooped up a pebble and sent it skipping expertly across the waves. It did fine until an incoming breaker claimed it. No, it wasn't the wedding that was worrying him. Flynn picked up another pebble and considered how perfectly things were falling into place.

He had everything he wanted, everything he needed to lay the foundation for the future. Angie, the dagger, which he strongly suspected Julian would give him for a wedding present, and a start in land investment. The future lay before him, ready and waiting.

So why was his intuition warning him that something was missing?

The second pebble lost its rhythm on the first skip and fell into the sea without a trace. Flynn shrugged and turned to walk back toward Julian's house.

Three days before the wedding Julian sprang his surprise party. Angie, who had been warned in advance, was there to see Flynn's startled expression as he walked through the front door of Julian's home and found the partygoers assembled inside.

Angie blew her intended a kiss over the heads of the small group of men Julian had invited, and then she picked up the car keys and went outside to drive herself to the cottage. Flynn could use Julian's car when he was ready to leave this evening. Unless, of course, he was too drunk to drive home.

It would be amusing to see Flynn Challoner tipsy,

Angie decided as she drove back to the cottage. She'd never seen him when he hadn't been in full control of himself. Unless she counted those two occasions when she'd lain in his arms. And his control was such that, even though she knew he desired her, he had been able to limit himself to those two occasions. Perhaps she'd feel more confident going into her marriage if she knew that in one area, at least, Flynn wasn't able to exert such control around her.

She thought about those two occasions off and on for the rest of the evening as she puttered around the cottage. In another three days she would be married. There was something unreal about the image. Flynn, himself, was as solid as granite and her own love for him was equally tangible. But the nagging wish for something more persisted.

She was as greedy as Maria Isabel had been. In the back of her mind Angie could almost see the other woman smiling in gentle commiseration. But she was also as reckless. She would take her chances with love.

At eleven o'clock Angie went to bed. A glance out the window revealed no lights on at the hacienda. Apparently the groom's party was still in full swing at Julian's. Angie pulled on her high-necked, long-sleeved flannel nightgown and turned back the bed. Before sliding under the quilt she cast a thoughtful look at the Torres Dagger, which lay on her dresser. Flynn had left it with her the night she'd pretended to toss it into the sea. When she'd mentioned its new location to her uncle, Julian had told her to keep it until the wedding.

"Why?" Angie had asked, astonished. She had been going to replace it in the cabinet in his study.

"I think you know why," Julian had said calmly. "The dagger goes with the Challoner bride."

If Flynn noticed that the dagger hadn't been returned to Julian's study, he said nothing about it.

She looked at the weapon now, moving over to the dresser to pick it up and gaze at the stones in its handle. Although she had clung to it tenaciously during the flight out of Mexico, threatened to hurl it into the sea during a moment of outrage and had it nearby for several days, she hadn't actually studied it in great detail. It was a lethal-looking thing. Could Maria Isabel have ever really intended to use it on her husband? It didn't make any sense, not now in light of what Angie was certain the other woman had been thinking on the eve of her wedding. But perhaps that was her own twentieth-century fantasies at work, Angie thought. It was risky trying to second-guess what a woman of that long-ago era had actually planned.

Setting the dagger down carefully, Angie turned out the light and climbed into bed. She had expected to lie awake, half listening for Flynn's return. She would be able to hear the car as it pulled into the hacienda drive.

An hour later it wasn't the sound of a car's engine that awakened her. It was a much smaller, far more significant sound. It was the soft noise of her living room door being opened.

A burst of excitement went through her. Flynn had returned, and instead of heading for his lonely bed at the hacienda, he had decided to spend the night with her. Wide awake, Angie pushed back the covers and climbed out of bed. Would he be very intoxicated, she wondered? She smiled to herself and went softly to the door of her bedroom.

It was as she stood there listening in the dark, trying to determine just how far gone her midnight visitor was, that a couple of things registered on Angie's brain.

The first was that she hadn't heard Flynn's car, or any car. Had he walked all the way back from Julian's? He might have if he thought he wasn't fit to drive. But the second fact hit her an instant later. If Flynn was too drunk to drive, that certainly wasn't him moving about so stealthily in her living room. She strained to hear and caught the soft, gliding sound of a foot dragging slightly on the carpet. With a flash of cold fear she remembered where she'd heard that particular gliding footstep before.

It had been the sound made by the person who had invaded her room that night in the Mexican hotel. Slowly Angie backed away from the door, horror making her almost numb for a few seconds. The gliding sound came again. Whoever it was, he was systematically going through her living room. Soon he would head down the hall to her bedroom. It was, after all, a very small cottage.

Spinning around, Angie grabbed a coat out of the closet, trying desperately not to make any noise. She knew what the intruder wanted, and she was equally certain he would not get his hands on it. She picked up a pair of sandals, not daring to take the time to put them on and then she went over to the dresser and took hold of the Torres Dagger.

There would be some noise when she went out the window, but Angie could see no alternative. Even now there was a sound from the hall. The man who had invaded her home was opening a closet door. She caught a quick stab of light and realized he must be carrying a flashlight.

Panic made her movements jerky. The window slid open with a soft, rasping sound and Angie tumbled through it, not knowing if whoever was in the hall had heard the noise.

An instant later she was on the ground, running blindly for the cliff path. In the dark a stranger might not find it. She might be able to hide down on the beach.

A light flashed behind her just as she reached the top of the path. Fear that she had been spotted sent her headlong down the unstable, pebbled surface. Her feet were already scratched and probably bleeding but she didn't dare take time to put on her sandals.

Halfway down the cliff she heard a shout in Spanish. She scrambled behind a rocky outcrop and glanced back, terrified of what she would see.

"The dagger, lady. All I want is the dagger. Give it to me and I'll go away and leave you alone."

She knew that voice but in her frozen state of mind, Angie couldn't quite place it. The light danced along the top of the cliff, sliding over the outcrop behind which she hid, and continued beyond it. He was searching for the route she had taken, she realized. If she emerged from behind her rocky cover and continued down the path he was likely to spot her. She had no choice but to stay where she was.

Trapped, Angie bent down to put on her sandals. It was hard to juggle the dagger and the jacket she had snatched from the closet. She shrugged into the jacket and shoved the blade of the dagger into an inside pocket. When the time came to run she would need both hands free.

The bobbing light paused at a point midway along the cliff, and Angie held her breath. She had a horrible premonition that whoever pursued her had found the way down the cliff.

Her breath seemed far too loud in the darkness, but she couldn't quiet it. The adrenaline pumping through her system was making her shake. Any action was preferable to none. Her scrabbling fingers found purchase on a large chunk of driftwood that had been flung high on the rocks during a storm. For some reason she found herself clinging to it as if she were caught in another kind of storm.

Then the light began to move purposefully, and Angie knew that the man had found the path. He would have trouble following it, but if he was careful and took his time, he'd probably make it down to the beach. In doing so he would pass right in front of her. Angie's fingers tightened on the length of driftwood.

As she waited, following his progress by the zigzagging motion of the flashlight, Angie prayed for loose pebbles and slippery sand. There were several curses in Spanish, a few missteps, but no major accidents. Her pursuer was going to make it down the path at least as far as her hiding point.

She would have to do something. Shrinking back against the cold rock surface, Angie clutched the driftwood and waited. She only had another few seconds.

Then time ran out. A shadowed, hulking form loomed up out of the darkness not more than a foot away. Angie swung the long stick of driftwood with all her might.

There was a muffled shout, a frantic scrabbling and then the sound of a body falling out of control down the steep path. Angie held her breath. The flashlight sailed outward, landing soundlessly in the sand below. A moment later something struck heavily and then there was silence.

Angie had no way of knowing how much damage she had done. She might have knocked the man unconscious, or she might only have unbalanced him and stunned him. It was even possible that the man had been killed in the fall. The thought made her sick to her stomach. In any event, common sense told her she shouldn't stick around to find out.

The hem of her nightgown whipped around her legs as she darted out from behind the outcrop and started climbing quickly up the path to the top of the cliff. Her hands were bruised and dirty by the time she reached the top.

Breath coming painfully between her teeth, Angie

ran toward the cottage. She dashed through the front door and raced across the room to the table where she normally tossed her car keys. They were gone. The intruder had probably pocketed them when he'd canvased her living room. There was no time to search. Remembering the spare key in the glove compartment, Angie dashed back outside to the car.

Too late she realized she'd never replaced the hidden key. It had been left on the same table as the regular set and now it, too, was gone.

"Idiot!" Railing at herself, knowing that this sort of thing probably never happened to Jake Savage and certainly not to Flynn Challoner, Angie made the next decision. She didn't dare stay around the cottage. If the man lying at the base of the cliff revived, that would be the first place he'd head. Picking up the skirts of her nightgown, Angie ran for the darkened hacienda. It was a big home with lots of closets and rooms in which to hide.

And the telephone had finally been installed earlier this week, she recalled as she arrived, out of breath, at the back door. The hacienda doors would all be locked, but Angie had no hesitation about picking up a rock and using it to shatter the small bathroom window.

Scrambling awkwardly, the sheathed knife biting into the flesh of her stomach at one point, she made it through the broken window with only a couple of small nicks. Then she stopped, gasping for breath, and realized she dared not turn on any lights.

The phone. Where had Julian put it? There were two, as she recalled. One was in the master bedroom. Making her way carefully through the dark house, Angie groped her way to the bedroom Flynn had been using.

It was then that she heard the sound of her uncle's car in the drive. Flynn was home.

The wave of relief was enough to make her dizzy. If there was anyone who would know what to do in a situation such as this, it would be Flynn. Angie turned back from the bedroom and raced down the hall. Flinging open the front door she saw the lights of the car switch off. A second later the car door opened.

"Flynn! Oh, my God, Flynn, thank heavens you're here. I've never been so glad to see anyone in my life." She dashed down the front steps to where he stood beside the car. "That man, the one from Mexico, the one who was in my room that night... He's here, Flynn. He's come for the dagger. But he didn't get it. I've got it and I, oh, Flynn, I hit him with a chunk of driftwood and I—"

"Angie, honey," Flynn breathed, starting toward her. "You're here."

"Well, of course I'm here. I mean, he took my car keys and I didn't have the spare, and I couldn't think of anything else—" She broke off, her mouth falling open in shock as she realized he wasn't paying any attention to her. Instead he was advancing on her with a determination that spelled only one thing.

"Flynn," she gasped, "how drunk are you?"

"Not too drunk to take you to bed," he assured her, his voice slurred and loud as he reached for her.

"No, wait a minute. You haven't been listening. We've got to get away from here...that man..." She struggled, aware of the alcohol on his breath. And to think she had thought it would be amusing to see Flynn intoxicated.

"Angie, honey," he growled, "stop wriggling. You don't have to wait any longer. I'm gonna take care of everything." His arms came around her in a huge, clumsy hug, and he began nuzzling her with awkward passion.

"Please, Flynn, listen to me! Stop it, I'm trying to tell you, I've got the dagger and we've got to get away..."

"Why do you always have to talk so much? After we're married you're gonna have to cut out all this chitchat. Won't tolerate it."

The warning was followed by another heavy kiss on her shoulder and then, so softly Angie didn't believe her ears, she heard him whisper, "Where's the dagger?"

Stunned, she tried to pull back. "Flynn..."

"The dagger," he rasped directly into her ear.

"Inside my jacket."

And then his hand was groping heavily inside the jacket opening in what must have looked like a clumsy caress. Angie froze as she felt him pluck the dagger from its hiding place.

What happened next was almost too fast for her to follow. Angie was freed abruptly as Flynn stepped back, swung around in a smooth, tight half circle and flung the dagger.

The scream of pain that came from off to one side

of the hacienda startled Angie so much she screamed in reaction.

"Flynn! What happened? How did you know he was there?"

Recovering from her shock, Angie hurried after Flynn, who was loping toward his victim. The man lay huddled on the ground, groaning in agony. The Torres Dagger was embedded in his right shoulder. There was a gun lying beside him. He'd evidently dropped it when the dagger had struck.

"I saw him at about the same time you came running down the steps dressed in that sexy little nightie." Flynn crouched to examine the man.

Angie glanced down at her cotton flannel gown and the jacket she wore over it. "This is hardly a sexy little nightie!" And then she wondered how she could possibly be offended at a time like this.

"On you it looks good," he told her absently. "Come here and give me a hand."

Angie went closer cautiously, peering at the face revealed in the watery moonlight.

"Good grief. It's Alexander Cardinal's gorilla butler."

At that moment the phone inside the hacienda started ringing.

"You'd better answer it. Must be your uncle," Flynn instructed as he examined the wounded man's shoulder. "Maybe he's calling to see if I got home okay."

Angie raced inside, grabbed the phone and listened in amazement to Julian's terse warning.

"In Jake Savage's immortal words, you're a little

late, Uncle Julian. But not to worry. Everything's under control.''

Then she slammed down the receiver and dashed outside.

''Julian says he's just had the most amazing call from Alexander Cardinal. Cardinal's in L.A. at the airport. He phoned Uncle Julian to warn him that Haslett might be coming after the dagger.''

''The warning's a little late, but it looks like everything's under control,'' Flynn said absently.

Angie blinked. ''Spoken like Jake Savage.''

Ten

Alexander Cardinal was as refined and elegant as ever as he sat sipping Mrs. Akers's excellent coffee the next morning. He had already succeeded in charming the housekeeper by asking her in a stage whisper if she would care to move to his island home. He wasn't sure he would be able to survive now without her coffee.

He had driven up from L.A. in a rented Lincoln Continental that matched his tropical white suit, and he looked right at home on the California coast. Like something off a movie set, perhaps, but right at home.

That was the wonderful thing about California, Angie thought in amusement as she stirred cream into her own coffee. It could accommodate so many different types.

Her uncle and Cardinal had hit it off at once.

Their lengthy correspondence concerning the dagger had already introduced them, and in person they found even more to discuss. As the two men solemnly considered the qualities of the steel used in such weapons as the Torres Dagger, Angie caught Flynn's eye.

It wasn't difficult to do. Flynn had barely let her out of his sight since last night. By the time the gorilla had been turned over to the authorities, it was almost two in the morning. Angie had been keyed up and exhausted. The combination had made it difficult to even think about sleeping. Flynn had hovered over her, continually demanding to know if she was really all right. He had bathed the small wounds she had acquired in her flight toward the cliff and then he had tried to fill her full of sherry.

"For your nerves," he'd said.

"My nerves are fine," she'd told him, trying to refuse the second glass.

"Then give me the sherry. Mine are shot to hell!"

There had been no question of where she would spend the night. Without bothering to discuss the subject, Flynn had tucked her into his bed at the hacienda and then slid in beside her. There had also been no question about doing anything other than sleeping. In spite of her inner tension, Angie had found the comfort of Flynn's arms was all she needed to sleep. She had gone out like a light and had not awakened until rather late. Flynn was already in the shower when she awoke. They had hurried to her uncle's house for breakfast and to await the arrival of Alexander Cardinal.

Angie was considering a second cup of coffee when the intent conversation between her uncle and Cardinal finally broke off. Cardinal smiled graciously at her.

"Julian tells me that you and Flynn will be marrying the day after tomorrow, Miss Morgan. Please accept my congratulations. And my apologies for the trouble Haslett gave you last night. Hardly an appropriate wedding gift. You're quite certain you're all right?"

"She's fine," Flynn answered for her with an edge of aggression underlying his words. "But I've got a few questions."

Faint mockery touched Cardinal's eyes. "Somehow I suspected you might. You are not a man to leave any loose threads dangling, are you, Flynn?"

"I left one hanging down in Mexico and look what happened."

"You refer to that unpleasant incident with the owner of the boat who tried to kidnap you." Cardinal nodded. "Yes, perhaps it would have been better if you had mentioned the matter to me before you left. But I suppose that at the time you thought I might have been the one to hire the man in the first place?"

"The thought crossed our minds," Flynn agreed. "It didn't make sense that anyone else would want the dagger that badly. On the other hand," he admitted dryly, "it didn't make any sense that you'd want it back, either. After all, you had been well paid and no one had forced you to agree to the deal in the first place."

"Loose ends," Cardinal repeated thoughtfully. "You are right, Flynn. Questions should be answered before they become dangerous. Actually it was your friend Ramon who first alerted me to the fact that I had a problem with Haslett. Rumors reached me that a cousin of a certain desk clerk at the resort had taken on a small job for me. Since I had never hired this cousin to do any small jobs, I became curious. Eventually I figured out that it was Haslett who had hired him, using my name for clout. My curiosity grew when the rumors implied it might have been you who left Ramon so embarrassingly tied up in a deserted cove. There must have been an interesting scene on board the boat that night."

"Memorable," Angie put in blandly.

Cardinal chuckled. "I can imagine. Well, I learned the two of you were safe and out of the country, so I made the mistake of not being overly concerned for your future safety. I know Haslett very well, you see. He has worked for me for years. Even if he was the one responsible for trying to grab the dagger, I was sure he wouldn't be able to follow you out of Mexico. And besides, I would know at once if he left the country. All in all, I was curious to find out if he was running some small scam on the side without my knowledge, but I wasn't concerned for Miss Morgan or the dagger. Whatever attempt had been made to steal it had obviously gone awry. I wasn't expecting another."

"But you continued to look into the possibility of Haslett having outside activities?" It was Julian who asked, his eyes betraying his keen interest. Angie had seen that expression before. Julian was doing more than satisfying his curiosity. He was collecting material for a Jake Savage novel. Writers had one-track minds.

Cardinal nodded. "I began making discreet inquiries and took a closer interest in Haslett's comings and goings. I learned recently that he was having clandestine meetings at the resort with a representative of a, shall we say, business conglomerate headquartered in Colombia."

"Cocaine deals?" Angie asked instantly.

Cardinal arched a handsome brow. "That was a fast connection, Miss Morgan."

"She does too much research for Julian," Flynn put in dryly. "Was it cocaine?"

"To tell you the truth, I do not know. I did not ask when I arranged to meet with this businessman. A man's business is largely his own affair, after all."

"You met with him?" Angie was startled.

"Of course. I wanted to know exactly what was going on. He explained that Haslett owed him a certain sum of money for a deal that had gone sour. I then told this businessman that I would pay my employee's debt. In return I expected that no further business deals would be conducted with Haslett."

"This, uh, businessman agreed?" Julian asked.

"All he wanted was his money. I gave it to him. Then I went home to have an employer-employee chat with Haslett. Unfortunately, I discovered that he had taken advantage of my absence to leave Mexico. A check with the airline people told me he was on his way to Los Angeles. And at that point, Flynn, I began to worry that he might still have dreams of getting hold of the Torres Dagger. He would have assumed the weapon was in Julian's home but when he arrived and found the party going on he must have decided to seek out Miss Morgan and use her in some way. Or perhaps he just hoped to get lucky and find the dagger, itself, in her home. Who knows?''

Angie poured herself more coffee. ''The poor guy didn't know you'd gotten him off the hook with the Colombian outfit. He must have been terrified. He was in trouble with a dangerous man. Colombian gangsters have a particularly nasty reputation.''

''Yes,'' Cardinal agreed simply. ''They do. I blame myself for not having acted more swiftly in this. But I honestly did not expect Haslett to be so desperate for the dagger that he would follow it back to the States. After all, it is a beautiful weapon and has great sentimental value to a Torres or it seems, a Challoner, but, frankly, its sale on the open market would not have raised enough to pay off Haslett's debt to the Colombian group.''

''So why has he fixated on getting it back?'' Flynn got to his feet, moving restlessly toward a window. He stood staring out to sea for a moment, his expression thoughtful. ''Unless he assumed it was worth more than it is?''

''I'm afraid that is precisely what he assumed. I do not discuss my financial deals with my employees. He did not realize that the dagger had more sentimental and historical value than commercial value. Haslett saw a dagger embedded with jewels and knew that I had made a deal to sell it. He assumed the weapon was very valuable. He would not know the difference between a ruby, say, and a garnet unless someone told him. All he knew was that he badly need a quick source of cash. To give Haslett his due, he would never have actually stolen the dagger from me.''

''But once you had sold it off to someone else, the dagger was fair game as far as he was concerned, right?'' Flynn looked at Cardinal.

''Exactly. Apparently poor Haslett could think of no other ready source of cash. He convinced himself he had to have that dagger. He thought it would be a simple matter at first. When the attempt to retrieve it in Mexico failed, he panicked and followed you.''

Julian's eyes lit up with an inspirational thought. ''Maybe we're the ones who don't know the difference between rubies and garnets. Perhaps over the years the semiprecious stones have been switched with diamonds and rubies and emeralds!''

Cardinal laughed. ''Trust a writer of adventure to come up with that possibility. I must tell you, however, that I had the weapon properly appraised when I first purchased it. I would not have sold it to you for the price I did if the stones had been more valuable. I pride myself on being a gentleman, but I'm afraid I am also a businessman.''

''Ah, well, just a thought,'' Julian said, clearly a little disappointed.

Angie spoke up again. ''What happens to Haslett now?''

Cardinal looked at her. "He is in the hands of your criminal justice system. He will have to take his chances with it."

"But you'll hire him a good lawyer?" she asked shrewdly.

"Yes. I will hire him a lawyer. The best. I am sorry if that offends you, Miss Morgan, but I really feel I have no choice."

"Of course you don't," Angie said with total understanding. "He's a longtime employee and until now he's been reliable. Apparently he got himself in over his head but if he doesn't have a history of unreliability you're right to take care of him. I approve of enlightened employers who feel some sense of obligation toward their employees." She paid no attention to Flynn's disgusted exclamation. She knew how Cardinal felt. He was from the old, paternalistic school of employers. There weren't many around these days.

"You seem to understand the situation from my point of view," Cardinal said to Angie. "Perhaps that is a legacy of your family's traditional sense of obligation to its employees?"

"It's a legacy from my years in personnel work. The only employee my family has had in recent years was the kid who cut the grass once a week! Unless you count Mrs. Akers."

"But the Torres and Challoner families must have been quite extensive. I understood their holdings took in much of this part of California. Surely there would have been many employees."

"That was a long time ago," Angie said with a

smile. "The families aren't quite what they used to be in terms of money or land, let alone employees."

Flynn swung around from the window, his eyes challenging. "But Angie and I are going to combine the two families again and rebuild, aren't we, Angie?"

She looked at him. "Yes, I guess we are." She turned toward Cardinal. "You'll stay for the wedding?"

Cardinal appeared genuinely pleased. "I would enjoy that very much. I like family gatherings, and it has been a long time since I attended a wedding. Perhaps that is because people no longer seem to marry for the right reasons."

Angie changed the subject.

Two evenings later Angie slipped into the lace-trimmed peignoir her mother had bought her. She twirled in a small circle in front of the dressing room mirror and watched with pleasure as the silky material floated enticingly around her ankles. Out in the master bedroom of the hacienda she could hear Flynn moving around, preparing for bed.

The wedding had gone off beautifully, of course. With Flynn attending to every detail there was no way anything could have gone awry. The champagne had been the best, the caviar was sturgeon and had been magnificently displayed on an ice sculpture, the flowers had been huge and brilliant, and the vast quantities of food prepared by Mrs. Akers had been hailed with grand enthusiasm by the assembled guests.

Few people knew the groom personally, but everyone had been prepared by Julian to meet Jake Savage's alter ego.

"Good for book sales," Julian had confided to Angie. "Look at the guests. They love him."

"They love adventure heroes, you mean," Angie had said knowledgeably.

"With Flynn they're getting the real thing. The story of how he drove home after his groom's party the other night and wound up using the Torres Dagger on the villain chasing you has already made the rounds. It's even been embellished a bit."

"How's that?" she demanded.

Julian grinned. "They're saying he pulled off the feat even though he'd had a considerable amount to drink at the party."

"I wondered about that myself. How much did Flynn drink that night?"

"No more than he could handle, apparently." Julian refused to say more on the subject.

The wedding had taken place on the grounds of the hacienda, and after the solemn ceremony things had turned cheerfully boisterous. Angie had begun to wonder if people would ever leave. Flynn hadn't encouraged anyone to hurry off. He was obviously enjoying his wedding.

Her mother had been thoroughly charmed by the groom, who had made it clear he had a great sense of family feeling.

"So many men don't these days," Mrs. Morgan had observed to her daughter. "They live only for themselves and the present. Your Flynn seems to be aware of what's truly valuable in life. He'll make you a fine husband, my dear.''

Angie hadn't argued. She'd simply had another glass of champagne and considered how Maria Isabel had felt at her wedding. It, too, had been a grand, boisterous affair with plenty of food and expensive wine. The guests hadn't left until three days later. Eventually, though, during the gala party following the ceremony, the groom had snagged his bride, swung her up in front of him on a huge bay stallion and taken her home. Maria Isabel had been nervous, excited and very much in love. The Torres Dagger had been secretly strapped to her arm beneath the flowing sleeve of her gown.

No one had told Angie the details of Maria Isabel's wedding. They were not part of the stories that had been handed down through the years. But as she dressed for her own wedding night, Angie knew many of those details, right down to the color of Curtis Challoner's big stallion. And she knew exactly how Maria Isabel had felt as she walked from the dressing room into Challoner's bedroom. Running a brush through her hair and checking her flushed expression in the mirror one more time, Angie prepared to make the same walk. Her fingers trembled slightly as she opened the door.

Flynn was still dressed, pacing the room like a large, restless cat. He stopped when he saw her standing in the doorway, his eyes going over her with a hunger that was shadowed with another emotion. Longing? Uncertainty? Doubt? Angie couldn't put a name to it and it alarmed her so much she couldn't move from the protection of the doorway.

"Flynn? What's wrong?"

"I wasn't sure until this afternoon," he told her starkly.

Angie felt her insides tighten with sudden anxiety. "Sure about what?"

"I've known for several days now that there was something missing from the equation. I thought I had it all put together. Everything I needed to start my family. Things should have been perfect."

"And they're not?" Her mouth felt dry.

"No," he grated, "they're not." He moved, taking a couple of the catlike, restless steps and stopped again.

"The dagger," she began desperately.

"Oh, the hell with the dagger. That's not the important thing."

Angie blinked at that. "What is the important thing, Flynn?"

"You."

"You've got me. Are…are you telling me you don't want me?"

He stared at her as if she'd lost her mind. "I want you so much it's tearing me apart."

"But, Flynn…"

He shifted abruptly, coming forward to stand only a foot away. Looking down into her wide, dismayed gaze, he shook his head slowly. "Lady with the peacock eyes. Why did you marry me?"

"I've told you," she began carefully. He didn't let her finish.

"You've told me all the reasons I gave you. Compatibility, a sense of history, mutual respect."

"Yes."

He drew a deep breath. "It's not enough."

"Not enough?" Hope flared in her, only to be followed by fear.

"That's the realization I've had this past week. It's been building in me, gnawing at me, eating me alive. This afternoon when we took our vows it all crystalized. Angie, I wanted you to marry me because you loved me. Not for any of those other reasons. I want you to love me as much as I love you."

"Do you love me, Flynn?" she asked softly.

"If I didn't I wouldn't be going through this anguish. I wouldn't have had so many doubts this past week. Honest to God, Angie, I thought I was going crazy at times. I couldn't figure out what was wrong with me and with my plans."

"Until today?"

He nodded. "I'm a slow learner, I guess. I had my head filled with all my schemes for rebuilding the family and for getting the marriage off on to a good start. I was so busy making certain everything fit together perfectly and all along there was something missing. I told myself that I had everything I needed from you, including passion. But it wasn't enough. Angie, I love you. And I won't rest until you've learned to love me, too."

She smiled tremulously. "I told you once that I'd only marry for love."

He inclined his head once in grim acceptance. "I had no right to—"

"I didn't change may mind, Flynn."

Flynn searched her face. "What are you saying?"

She pushed back the sleeve of her gown and revealed the Torres Dagger. "I love you, Flynn. I've loved you almost from the beginning. Women such as Maria Isabel and myself only marry for the right reason: love."

"Angie?" He stared at the dagger as she held it out to him, hilt first.

"Take the dagger, Flynn. I'm giving it to you the same way Maria Isabel gave it to your ancestor."

"I don't understand," he whispered, slowly taking the dagger from her hand.

"Everyone has always assumed Maria Isabel took that dagger with her on her wedding night with the intention of using it on her husband. She didn't. She took it to give to him as a symbolic act. In those days a combatant surrendered his sword to the victor of the battle. Maria Isabel had no sword, but she wanted Curtis to know that she intended to end the war. She was his wife, and she had married him because she loved him. Surrendering the dagger was her way of telling him. I'm giving it to you for the same reason: because I'm your wife and that dagger is symbolic of all that's been between us. It's yours. I'm yours. I love you."

"Angie... Oh, God, *Angie.*"

He pulled her close, cradling her against his chest, whispering his broken words of love. She clung to him, cherishing the moment of commitment, drawing the certainty of his love deep into her heart.

"This is the way it's supposed to be," Flynn said.

She lifted her head to smile mistily. "I know."

He held her fiercely for a moment longer, and then Flynn released her abruptly. He was grinning with enthralling wickedness.

"Flynn Challoner, what are you doing?"

"Following an old family tradition!" He picked up one of the dress shoes he'd bought for the wedding, kicked a footstool over in front of the fireplace and leaped up on it, the dagger in his fist. "Hand me the sheath. Some carpenter left a couple of nails here on the mantel."

"I'm not sure we need to carry tradition this far," Angie said warily as she obediently handed him the dagger's old leather sheath.

But Flynn was already using the heel of the shoe to pound a nail into the wall. He hung the sheath, inserted the dagger and leaned back proudly to survey the results. "There's a lot to be said for tradition."

He jumped down from the footstool and scooped Angie up in his arms. Swinging her around in an abandoned whirl, he carried her over to the bed and dropped her down in the center.

Angie steadied herself and laughed up at him. "And now what, Challoner?"

"Now this upstart peasant is going to do you a favor, lady." He peeled off his shirt and unbuckled his belt. "I'm going to make you into a loving wife." The rest of his clothing fell to the floor.

"Ah, but Challoner, I already am a loving wife." Leaning back against the pillows Angie opened her arms to him.

"Show me." The laughter left his eyes, to be replaced by hungry appeal. "Please show me, Angie."

Angie had never seen him look so vulnerable. Tenderly she drew him down to her. "I love you, Flynn. I will be happy to go on demonstrating that for the rest of our lives." And then her promise was swallowed up in the depths of his kiss. Love laced with vibrant passion blazed between a Challoner and a Torres just as it had on a similar wedding night in the long ago past.

Back at Julian's home, Alexander Cardinal poured another glass of fine Spanish sherry and toasted his host and the mother of the bride.

"I don't know when I've enjoyed myself more. I believe I'll come back for the christening."

"Christening?" Mrs. Morgan asked, startled.

"You don't think Flynn's going to waste any time founding the dynasty, do you?"

When Curtis Torres Challoner was born nine months later, Alexander Cardinal was there to celebrate. He was invited to stay at the new home Flynn Challoner had just finished building for his small family and during the tour of the house he was allowed a glance into the master bedroom.

The Torres Dagger was hung proudly over the fireplace.

* * * * *

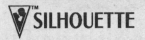

Reader Service™

The best romantic fiction direct to your door

Our guarantee to you...

The Reader Service involves you in no obligation to purchase, and is truly a service to you!

Your books are delivered hot off the press, at least one month before they are available in the shops.

Your books are sent on 14 days no obligation home approval.

We offer free postage and packing for subscribers in the UK—we guarantee you won't find any hidden extras.

Plus, we have a dedicated Customer Care team on hand to answer all your queries on
(UK) 0181 288 2888
(Ireland) 01 278 2062.
There is also a 24 hour message facility on this number.

LINDA HOWARD

DIAMOND BAY

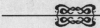

Someone wanted this man dead. He was barely alive as
he floated up to the shore. Shot twice and unconscious.
Rachel's sixth sense told her she was his only hope.
The moment she decided not to call the police
she decided his future. As well as her own.

"Howard's writing is compelling."

—Publishers Weekly

1-55166-307-4
AVAILABLE IN PAPERBACK
FROM DECEMBER, 1998

FIND THE FRUIT!

Do you know your fruit? If you do then you are one step ahead when it comes to completing this puzzle, because all the answers are fruit! Here's what you have to do…

There are ten coded words listed underneath, which when decoded each spell the name of a fruit. There is also a grid which contains each letter of the alphabet and a number has been provided under some of the letters. Complete the grid by working out which number corresponds to each letter of the alphabet. When you have done this, you will be able to decipher the coded words to discover the names of the ten fruit!

A	B	C	D	E	F	G	H	I
15					20			

J	K	L	M	N	O	P	Q	R
	25						5	

S	T	U	V	W	X	Y	Z
			10				

4	19	15	17	22

15	10	3	17	15	18	3

2	19	17	8	15	6	23	2	19

4	19	15	6

4	26	9	1

7	8	6	15	11	16	19	6	6	13

3	6	15	2	21	19

15	4	4	26	19

1	15	2	21	3

16	15	2	15	2	15

ANSWERS: A=15, B=16, C=17, D=18, E=19, F=20, G=21, H=22, I=23, J=24, K=25, L=26, M=1, N=2, O=3, P=4, Q=5, R=6, S=7, T=8, U=9, V=10, W=11, X=12, Y=13, Z=14.